Ethan turned to me, and I looked up at him.

We were standing so close I could smell the peppermint from the gum he'd been chewing.

And at that moment I knew. I just knew. He was going to kiss me.

I lifted my chin and closed my eyes, ready for the moment I had dreamt about, wondered about, and secretly practiced for with my pillow at night.

His lips were just about on mine, everything was perfect, when suddenly, there she was.

"Dixie! Dixie! I brought you some food!" Patti yelled, stumbling through the trees toward us. . . .

CLUB Sunset Island™

DIXIE'S FIRST KISS

CHERIE BENNETT

SPLASH™

B

A BERKLEY / SPLASH BOOK

DIXIE'S FIRST KISS is an original publication of The Berkley Publishing Group. This work has never appeared before in book form.

DIXIE'S FIRST KISS

A Berkley Book / published by arrangement with General Licensing Company, Inc.

PRINTING HISTORY
Berkley edition / July 1994

A GLC BOOK

Splash, Sunset Island and Club Sunset Island are trademarks belonging to General Licensing Company, Inc.

ISBN: 0-425-14291-4

BERKLEY®
Berkley Books are published by The Berkley Publishing Group, 200 Madison Avenue, New York, New York 10016.
BERKLEY and the "B" design are trademarks belonging to Berkley Publishing Corporation.

PRINTED IN THE UNITED STATES OF AMERICA

10 9 8 7 6 5 4 3 2 1

For my darling

*The author also wishes to thank
Debbie Strichartz for
her assistance with
information about asthma.*

ONE

"Y'all, I have major news," I declared, running over to my three best friends, Becky and Allie Jacobs (they're identical twins) and Tori Lakeland.

We were all gathered at the campfire area, waiting for morning announcements to begin. I'd only met Becky, Allie, and Tori a few weeks before when we'd all begun our summer jobs as counselors-in-training at Club Sunset Island, but sometimes you just click with certain people, you know? Well, that's what happened with us. And when the camp was divided into two teams—the red team and the blue team—the four of us were all put on the red team. Now, that's what I call fate!

"I declare. That 'y'all' thing you do is just the cutest thing," Becky drawled, imitating my Southern accent. "It almost makes me wish I had a Southern accent, too."

"But Dixie is from Mississippi and you're from Long Island," Tori said seriously. "That wouldn't make any sense."

1

Allie, Becky, and I just shook our heads. Tori has a tendency to be kind of literal-minded.

"So, what's the dirt?" Allie asked me, scratching at a bug bite on her ankle.

"If it's about boys, I don't want to hear it," Tori warned, popping a chunk of bubble gum into her mouth.

"Well, it kind of is," I admitted. "But in this case—"

"Figures," Tori interrupted. "Do you think it's fair to talk about boys in front of a girl who is never, ever, *ever* going to have a boyfriend? Namely me."

"Hey, didn't Allie and I tell you we were going to give you boy lessons?" Becky reminded Tori.

"Tori, what I'm trying to tell you is—" I began.

"Hi, girls. How's it going?" Pete Tilly asked, coming over to us. Pete is fifteen, a senior counselor-in-training (the four of us are junior C.I.T.s, so he's kind of our boss), and he's very cute and nice.

"Oh, just terrif," Allie told him breezily. "Cool T-shirt," she added.

Pete had on a Real Men Don't Wear Fur T-shirt which featured thousands of eyes peeking out through a green jungle. Of course, I reckon if he'd had on a plain old white T-shirt Allie would have said the same thing. She *really* likes Pete Tilly.

"Thanks," Pete said. He turned to Tori. "Hey, I was in your parents' store yesterday to pick up *Greenpeace News*," he told her. "It's a great place."

Tori actually lives on Sunset Island—which is this resort island off the coast of Maine—all year round, whereas the rest of us are only here for summer vacation. Her parents own the local health food store. Maybe that's why Tori is a junk food junkie.

"Oh, well, uh . . . um . . ." Tori stammered.

"She's just being modest," I put in helpfully. Tori stammers something terrible when she gets around boys. Especially cute boys.

Pete smiled at her, and she tried to smile back, but just as she did, the gum she'd been chewing stuck to her lower lip. She reached up to pluck it off, and it stuck to her fingers. Then she tried to shake it off her fingers, but they just stuck together in a big old mess.

Pete took in Tori's antics and kind of swallowed a laugh. "See ya later," he said and took off.

"Please, just kill me now," Tori groaned, then she gnawed the rest of the gum off her sticky fingers. "I am hopeless. I am always going to be hopeless. I am never going to—"

"Tori Lakeland!" I yelled. "Hush up! I have been trying to tell you boy news that just happens to be bad news for me and good news for you!"

She stopped moaning and stared at me. "This is a joke, right?"

"Wrong," I countered. "A.J. called me last night, and he's got the flu." A.J. is this darling boy from Camp Eagle I had met a few days earlier when he and his friends got shipwrecked on our island during a storm. Tori had really hit it off with A.J.'s friend, Tim. And although Tim had asked for Tori's phone number, he hadn't called her and Tori was convinced he never would.

Tori looked at me blankly. "Why would I be glad that A.J. has the flu?"

"Tim has the flu, too," I continued. "In fact, he's sick as a dog. Which, according to A.J., is why he hasn't called you!"

Tori's eyes lit up. "You mean it? That's the only reason?"

I nodded.

"Well, I'll be," Tori marveled. "Although I'll believe it when my phone actually rings. Not that I'd know what to say to him if he actually called me. So I guess it doesn't matter if he doesn't call me, because I'd be, like, totally silent. That would be dumb, though, wouldn't it? Maybe I could talk about sports. If I practiced."

Tori also has a tendency to ramble on like this at times.

She furrowed her eyebrows. "So why is that bad news for you?"

"You remember A.J. invited me to Camp Eagle's dance on Friday night," I told her. "So, now we can't go because he's sick."

4

"So the four of us will have to do something radical Friday night instead," Becky declared.

Ethan Hewitt, this very cute boy who is a junior C.I.T. on the blue team, waved at me as he headed over to the other side of the campfire area. I waved back.

"He's crazed for you, you know," Allie told me.

"I like him, too," I said happily.

"I thought you liked A.J.," Tori reminded me.

"Well, I like them both," I decided. I grinned remembering something I'd heard from Samantha Bridges, the Jacobs twins' au pair: So many boys, so little time.

Just then, Bobby Babbit, who along with his wife Barbi was co-executive director of Club Sunset, blew his whistle to start morning announcements.

"Good morning, campers!" Bobby yelled into his megaphone. "Wow, is it a groovy morning, or what?"

I need to explain to you about Bobby and Barbi. They are in their forties, but I believe they left their hearts at Woodstock—you know, that rock love-in that took place sometime back in the dark ages?

Bobby went into his endless announcements and I let my mind drift off. I thought about how amazing it was that I was actually at Club Sunset working as a C.I.T. with the three most fabulous best friends in the universe.

I live light years away from Sunset Island, in

Starkville, Mississippi, which is so small that if you spit, the spit lands in another town.

Not that I would ever spit.

Even though I am only thirteen, I am a Southern Lady—at least that's what has been hammered into my head by my mother, who is Queen of the Southern Ladies. She is a professor of home economics at Mississippi State University and my father is a professor of psychology who does research on the human brain.

My mother is kind of famous in her own way. She wrote a book a few years back called *The Happy Homemaker*, all about the true joy of motherhood, wifehood, and matching your wallpaper to your coffee table. This book was a surprise bestseller, and my mother was on a lot of talk shows.

I always found this kind of amusing, since A) my mother teaches full time and does not stay at home to do what she promotes in her book, and B) when she traveled around to be on all these talk shows, she was home even less than that.

One thing my mother always wanted—in addition to a perfect home—was a beauty-queen daughter. My older sister, Crystal, and I both started out in the beauty-queen business when we were just bitty things. I even won America's Little Miss Sweetheart when I was seven. I tried to be perfect at it, just like Mom wanted, but the truth was I hated it. After that I refused to enter any more pageants. I just have no interest in that at all. Fortunately for my mother, my sister does. In fact, this year she is Miss Mississippi. That's right. She's competing in Atlantic City this fall.

It's a funny thing about how people judge other people. For example, because I'm petite and blond, because I'm a cheerleader and a baton twirler, and because I have a Southern accent, people often think I'm silly or dumb. Well, this just isn't true. I get all A's in school and I plan to become an astronaut. And I'll do it, too.

Of course, before I do that, I do want to break maybe a million or so hearts.

The truth is, I don't know much about breaking hearts. My parents are very, very, very strict. Let me add another "very" to that. I am not allowed to date until I'm eighteen. I can't even talk to a boy on the phone. Once I held hands with a boy and I was so scared my parents would find out that I had a major asthma attack and had to go to the hospital.

I suppose one of the reasons my parents are so strict is because of my asthma. Asthma is a condition where your bronchial tubes constrict, making it really difficult to breathe. Some people have mild cases of asthma and it doesn't bother them very much. My asthma is pretty serious. I mean, I've been in the hospital four times for it, which was really scary. I always carry this inhaler with me, and I use it when my lungs start to feel tight. The truth of the matter is, I find it embarrassing to use my inhaler in front of anyone, so I kind of try to hide it.

I know that asthma can be serious, but Lord, my parents treat it as if I could be heading to heaven every time I have a little cold or something. It's very icky. I swear they would keep me wrapped in cotton if they could, up on some shelf where they could just take me off to look at me once a day.

Well, with this kind of life you can imagine how eager I was to get away from home my last summer before ninth grade. (I'm a year ahead in school because I skipped fifth grade.) When my cousin, Molly Mason, invited me to spend the summer with her, I begged my parents until my face turned blue. Molly is sixteen, and she and her parents (her father is my father's brother) live on Sunset Island. Molly was in a terrible car accident, and now she's confined to a wheelchair. Anyway, I convinced my parents that I wanted to come to Sunset Island to help keep Molly company, and they finally bought into that.

Of course, that wasn't exactly the truth.

Molly—formerly known to her friends as Maniac Mason because of her daredevil ways—was the one who wanted to help out poor Dixie who had no life at all to speak of back in Starkville, Mississippi. Wonder of wonders, Molly and I actually pulled this all off, and here I am!

I looked over at Allie and Becky and I had to smile. They look just about exactly alike, except Becky has a beauty mark over her lip. Allie is more into outdoorsy things than Becky—Becky hates stuff like that. Also, Allie likes to read and she is always on some kind of spiritual quest. Becky likes taking care of the littlest kids at camp, which Allie can't stand. And Becky wants to be a singer and an actress.

The twins are fourteen and I am just in total awe over how sophisticated they are. They have had lots of dates and I think they must have kissed lots of boys already. They have really pretty long brown hair and big brown eyes. They are being raised by their dad, because their mom left when they were really little. (Whenever I feel like screaming over my mother I think about that, and then I feel lucky to have a mother, even if I have disappointed her by not continuing my career as a beauty queen.)

Tori is wonderful, too, in her own crazy way. She's as inexperienced with boys as I am. But whereas I love talking to them, she is just petrified. She is very cute (although she doesn't think so), with tons of long dark brown hair, and she's a wonderful athlete. She has a very big family and lots of pets. It always seems like her buttons are falling off or her shoelaces are broken, but that's just her style. In fact, she just loves wearing her old favorites to death.

If I walked around like that, my mother would

pitch a fit, but Tori's family is very relaxed about things like that.

The four of us seem so different from each other that I suppose people are surprised that we are so close. Today, for example, Becky had on tight jeans and a red T-shirt that laced up the back, and her hair was loose. Allie had on drawstring pants and a cropped denim shirt, and her hair was back in a braid. Tori had on oversized green shorts, a faded Grateful Dead tie-dyed T-shirt, and a Red Sox baseball cap worn backwards over a long ponytail. I had on a red and white striped T-shirt tucked into a pair of neat white shorts and a red ribbon in my hair. I was also wearing my lucky diamond tennis bracelet. (I'll tell you more about that later.)

"The first white-water rafting trip led by our fearless red team is going to be beautiful!" Bobby's voice boomed, snapping me out of my reverie. "Fearless red team" meant me and my friends, but I hadn't heard a word he'd said. "Just remember, you have to sign up for the trip by the end of the day," Bobby cautioned, "and you'll have to turn in permission slips signed by your parents by Wednesday. Have a far-out day at camp today, everybody!" he concluded enthusiastically.

"What did he say?" I asked Becky, as the group broke up to head off to our various scheduled activities. "Something about the red team leading a white-water rafting trip?"

"Doesn't that sound cool?" Allie asked with excitement.

"No," Becky replied. "It sounds wet."

"Oh, rafting is a blast," Tori said, as we headed to the pool to supervise a free swim.

"Girls, girls!" Barbi Babbit called, rushing over to us. Two girls were following her—a chubby camper who was struggling to keep up and a girl who looked about our age.

"We've got two terrific additions to the red team whom I want to introduce to you," she told us. She put her arm around the younger girl. "This is Patti Chernick—Patti's eleven years old, and she and her family just got to the island."

"Hi," I said, and Allie, Becky, Tori and I all introduced ourselves.

Poor thing. The girl hadn't said a word yet and I already felt sorry for her. Besides being chubby and shapeless, she had braces on her teeth, pale skin covered with freckles, and short black hair that stuck out in all directions. Patti gave me a shy, forlorn look, like a mongrel puppy hoping she won't get a whipping.

"Don't you have pretty eyes," I offered, which was true—they were a beautiful bright shade of blue—

and it was also the only honestly nice thing I could think of to say.

She smiled at me like I had just given her the moon with a fence around it. I smiled back and gave her arm a reassuring little squeeze.

"And this," Barbi continued in her breathless style, "is Delores De Witt. She's a senior C.I.T. like Pete, but she was in France with her parents so she's starting camp late."

"Call me Dee Dee," the girl said in a bored voice.

Barbi chattered on and I checked out Dee Dee. She was absolutely fabulous looking, with golden curls, huge blue eyes with long, sooty eyelashes and a great figure.

She also looked like she was just too bored to live.

"So, I'll leave all of you to rap and get to know each other," Barbi said gaily, and she walked away.

"Nice to meet you," I said to Dee Dee, since I am, as I said, a Well Brought Up Southern Young Lady and that is what we always say.

"I'm sure it is," Dee Dee said dryly, shifting her weight to her other foot.

Just at that moment, I happened to look over at Allie and Becky. Their faces had both gone completely white.

"You aren't . . . related to Diana De Witt by any chance, are you?" Allie asked nervously.

I remembered that name—Allie and Becky had

told me about Diana De Witt. She was the mortal enemy of their au pair, Samantha Bridges: nineteen, gorgeous, filthy rich, and according to the twins, the most malicious girl on the face of the earth.

"Yes, I am related to Diana," Dee Dee said, tossing her curls. "She's my cousin." A glint came into her eye. "Diana's from the poorer, *sweeter* side of the family."

Meaning that Dee Dee De Witt was richer and nastier than the nastiest girl on the face of the earth? And as a red team senior C.I.T. she was going to be one of our bosses!

I had a very bad feeling. We were about to be in as much trouble as a one-legged man in a butt-kicking contest.

TWO

Allie gave Dee Dee a level look. "So, if you're so rich, why would you want a job working with little kids?"

"It's not exactly my idea of a good time," Dee Dee said with a dramatic sigh. "Actually, I got into some trouble at my boarding school in Switzerland, so my parents packed me off here to spend the summer with Diana. She's supposed to be a good influence on me."

At this Becky and Allie looked even more distressed, if that was possible.

"My parents heard about this new camp, and they decided that a summer job would build my character," Dee Dee added, rolling her eyes.

"Hey, that's funny!" Tori exclaimed, her usual genial self. "That's the line all our parents used!"

Dee Dee didn't crack a smile. She looked down at Patti, who was still standing there, kind of rooted to the spot. "Don't you have some kiddies you need to run along and play with?" Dee Dee asked her.

"Not really," Patti replied honestly. "I mean, I don't know anyone here."

"Come on," I told her. "I'll take you over to the red team's free swim and introduce you around."

Patti smiled gratefully and put her sweaty hand in mine.

"I'll show Dee Dee around camp," Tori offered, popping another piece of gum into her mouth. I had to smile at Tori. She is friendly to absolutely *everyone*.

Dee Dee looked Tori over and raised one eyebrow. "Does that mean I'm supposed to actually be *seen* with you?" she asked.

"Don't worry," Tori replied with a laugh, "I'll tell everyone we meet that you're just looking over the country club to decide if you want to buy it or not."

As Tori and Dee Dee took off, Allie and Becky stifled a laugh, and then the three of us headed for the outdoor pool with Patti in tow.

"Have you ever been to camp before?" I asked Patti.

"No," she replied, looking nervous. She still held tightly to one of my hands, and she put the other hand over her stomach. "Oh boy, I think I need to go to the bathroom!"

"It's right over there," Allie said, pointing to the women's room door to the side of the pool.

Patti ran for it, clutching her stomach.

"Should we go after her?" I wondered.

"Nah," Becky decided. "She'll probably be embarrassed if we baby her."

16

"Y'all, I think she's really, really shy," I said. "We'll need to be extra nice to her."

"Thank you so much, Miss Congeniality," Becky teased me.

I made a face at her. "You know what I mean. Kids can be really cruel to a girl as scared and out of it as she is."

We stripped down to our bathing suits and laid our clothes on some chaise lounges. I had on a pink one-piece suit—very conservative—which is the only kind my parents will let me wear. I mean, I think if they could get me to swim in *armor* they would. The twins had on teeny, tiny polka-dot bikinis.

I sighed and stared enviously at those bathing suits. "I wish I had a bathing suit like that," I said.

"You can borrow one if you want," Becky offered.

"Please Becks," Allie scoffed. "She is a size three and we are a size seven," she reminded her twin.

"Well, there's so little material here, how can it matter?" Becky asked, pulling out some suntan lotion.

"I would need major cosmetic surgery before *my* top fit into *that* top," I pointed out, staring enviously at the well-developed twins.

"Girls, can you please supervise the diving competition while I entertain the kids in the kiddie pool?" Liza Ozur, our head counselor, asked us, two little kids hanging off each of her arms.

17

"Sure," Becky replied for us.

"Where's Tori?" Liza asked, looking around.

"She went to show Dee Dee around camp," I replied.

"Oh yeah, Dee Dee," Liza said, as if she had just remembered that Dee Dee existed. And she didn't sound any too happy about it, either.

"Well, tell Tori to help the intermediate kids with their butterfly and backstroke at the indoor pool when she gets back, okay?"

Patti ran back over to us from the ladies' room, tripping over her shoelaces and almost falling down in the process.

"You okay now?" I asked her.

She nodded. "Sometimes I have problems with my stomach when I get nervous," she admitted. "Sometimes my stomach even makes terrible noises. I keep pink stuff in my purse that I'm supposed to drink if my stomach gets upset."

To illustrate this, Patti opened her little purse and pulled out a bottle of pink medicine, which she swigged down like it was soda. It left a pink mustache around her mouth, which she tried to wipe away with the back of her hand.

"I always have to have this stuff with me," Patti insisted seriously.

"You missed some," Becky told her.

Patti swiped at her mouth again. "I bet my tongue

is all pink now, huh?" she asked, and stuck out her tongue.

It was, as promised, a hideously pink color.

"That always happens," she explained, tucking the bottle back into her purse.

"You could leave your purse inside the clubhouse," I suggested.

"Oh no," Patti said. "What if I need more medicine?"

I couldn't really argue with that. I mean, I always carry an inhaler in my back pocket, just in case I have an asthma attack. Though even *I* don't have it actually *on* me when I'm about to go swimming.

"Well, I doubt that you'll need it," I assured Patti. "You're going to have a wonderful time here!"

"Will you be my counselor?" Patti asked, clutching at my hand again. Her big eyes looked up into mine, even though she was almost as tall as I was.

"Sure," I promised, though I wished she'd give my hand a rest.

"Have fun, Patti," Becky told her, then she turned to me. "We'll meet you over by the high board." The twins took off for the diving pool.

I turned to Patti. "Do you have a bathing suit on?"

She nodded again, and awkwardly pulled her shorts and T-shirt off, tripping over her shoelaces again in the process. Her bathing suit was shocking pink with gigantic heart-covered ruffles around the midriff. It was a suit that would have been cute on a three year old, but not on a shy, chubby eleven year old.

"Nice bathing suit, Porky Pig," a boy hooted sarcastically as he ran by us. His friend guffawed loudly, and the two little monsters jumped into the pool, splashing wildly.

Patti looked like she was going to cry. She dropped my hand and attempted to cover up her body.

"Just ignore him," I advised Patti in a low voice. "There are plenty of nice kids here."

There are three outdoor pools at the club—the diving pool, the regular swimming pool, and the kiddie pool. There's also a huge indoor pool. I looked around the main outdoor pool for someone to introduce Patti to and I saw Jodie Graff, a twelve year old with the voice and attitude of a woman of the world. Her deep voice had something to do with the fact that she had serious heart and lung problems. She wasn't allowed to do a lot of the things the other kids did, like running or diving.

"Come on," I told Patti. She took my hand again and I led her over to Jodie, who was sitting by the side of the pool, dangling her legs in the water.

"Hey Jodie," I said.

Jodie was wearing a pair of Hollywood-style sunglasses and she was listening to a Walkman. She took off her headphones and put them around her neck. I could hear the heavy metal music blasting away.

"This is Patti Chernick," I told Jodie. "She's new. Patti, this is Jodie Graff."

Jodie nodded from behind her dark glasses. She bopped her head in time to the pounding bass line of her music.

"You like metal?" she asked Patti.

Patti plopped down next to her. "No. I don't like any kind of music," she said seriously.

"Get out of town," Jodie replied, lifting her sunglasses to give Patti a look of disbelief.

"Well, I went to an opera once," Patti recalled. "That was okay, although I think I'm probably a better singer than that lady. It wasn't a professional opera but it was in Italian. I speak Italian."

"Oh yeah, swell," Jodie said.

"I speak French and German, too," Patti added. "I have a very high IQ."

"Cool," Jodie replied, putting her earphones back on and her sunglasses back down.

Patti looked up at me. "She doesn't like me."

"Well, you two need a chance to get to know each other is all," I explained.

"Why is your voice so low?" Patti asked Jodie, yelling over the music blasting into Jodie's earphones.

"I smoke a lot of cigarettes," Jodie yelled back.

"I would never smoke," Patti said self-righteously. "It's a really stupid habit."

"Do tell," Jodie murmured.

21

"Smoking is very, very bad for you," Patti added.

"Yeah, well so's sugar, but I don't think that's stopping you," Jodie pointed out, eyeing Patti's ruffled midriff.

This wasn't going very well at all.

"See, I told you she didn't like me," Patti said, staring up at me forlornly. "Kids never like me."

"It's like I said, Patti," I explained, "I'm sure the two of you will get along just fine once you get to know each other."

"Not," Jodie snorted.

"So, I'll see y'all later!" I said cheerily, pretending I hadn't heard Jodie's negative assessment of Patti. I waved and backed away.

"Can I go with you?" Patti yelled to me.

"Uh, not now, honey," I replied.

"Why?"

"Because I have work to do," I said, trying to sound patient.

"So?" she yelled to me.

"So I have to go . . . do the work. Bye!"

I hurried around the corner toward the diving pool and I ran into Ethan Hewitt.

"Hi," he said. "Where are you headed?"

"The diving pool," I told him.

He leaned against the side of the building, as if he had all day. I figured that meant he wanted to talk with me. I couldn't help noticing how cute he looked. He had on jeans and a royal blue T-shirt. His reddish-brown hair fell over his forehead and he kept shaking it out of his eyes. I thought he looked kind of like a young version of Christian Slater.

"So, do you know how to dive?" he asked me.

"Not really," I admitted. "My dad tried to teach me last summer, but I got all chicken when I got up there on the board."

"It's not so tough," Ethan said casually. "I could probably teach you sometime."

"Really? That would be great!" I agreed.

He flicked his hair out of his eyes again. "So . . . I kind of volunteered to go on the white-water rafting trip with you guys."

"I thought it was just the red team leading it," I said.

"Yeah," Ethan agreed. "But they needed a couple more counselors because so many kids want to go."

"Have you ever gone rafting before?" I asked him.

"Nah," he admitted. "But I'm sure it's no big thing."

"I don't know," I said. "I've heard it can be really scary and dangerous—it depends on how big the rapids are."

Ethan shrugged. "Well, maybe we can be on the same raft or something."

"That would be nice," I agreed with a smile.

"Well, I have to go check out the blue team's volleyball game," Ethan said. "So, I'll see ya."

I hugged myself and ran to the diving pool, where the twins were helping to supervise a group of twelve year olds from both the red and the blue teams. Kids were working one at a time with Pam Tracey, the water sports specialist. The others were playing in the far end of the pool or standing around in groups talking by the side.

"Y'all, Ethan Hewitt is the cutest thing in the world," I told them happily.

"I thought A.J. was," Allie said.

"Well, they both are," I amended. I told them about the conversation I had just had with Ethan. "Do you think he's going on the rafting trip because of me?"

"For sure," Becky stated.

"Oh, that's so wonderful!" I cried.

"Winning the lottery is wonderful," Becky corrected me. "A white-water rafting trip cannot be wonderful."

"Oh, ignore her," Allie said. "Her idea of outdoor adventure is sitting in a hot tub. So, how'd it go with Patti?"

"She's not the most loveable girl I've ever met. I'll tell you that," I admitted.

"She's a nerd," Allie explained. "She might as well wear a sign that says 'I'm a nerd. Kick me.'"

"Poor thing," I murmured.

"Oh, I don't buy that," Becky said. "No kid has to be a nerd. She needs to get a life!"

"Well, y'all, that's why she's here at camp!" I pointed out. "We're supposed to *help* her get a life!"

"Yeah, I suppose," Becky agreed reluctantly.

"Okay, I've seen camp and it's just ducky," Dee Dee said, strolling over to us with Tori. "Now what?"

"Ask Liza," Becky told her.

"Oh, the head counselor," she recalled. She glanced up and happened to see Greg Racer, the head counselor for the blue team, walking by with Bobby Babbit. "I'd rather ask him," she said, looking Greg over.

"He's in college," Allie pointed out. "He's a little old for you."

Dee Dee laughed. "I doubt it."

"Besides, he's dating Liza," I added.

"For the moment, maybe," Dee Dee said coyly. "Well, I have to go make a phone call. I'll go check with Liza after that. . . . If I feel like it," she added before sauntering off.

The four of us watched her go.

"I have a bad feeling about her," Allie murmured.

"Y'all, we don't have to worry!" I exclaimed. "She

isn't going to do a lick of work, which means she'll get fired!"

"I don't think so," Tori said. "When we were walking around she told me that her uncle donated a lot of money to the club for the new wing. You know, where the little theater is and everything. She could sit around watching TV for the summer and she wouldn't get fired."

"Oh, just great," Becky groused. "Can you imagine what she's going to be like on the rafting trip? She'll probably expect us to carry her and her raft around on our shoulders."

"Maybe she'll lighten up," Tori said with a shrug. She blew a huge bubble with her gum and popped it with her tongue. "She's really pretty, huh?"

"Only if you like perfection," Allie snorted.

"Well, I'm not wasting my time worrying about her," I decided, jumping up from the side of the pool. "I'm going down to the kiddie pool to see if Liza needs more help."

I walked the long way to the kiddie pool so that I could go by the spot where I'd left Patti and Jodie. I just hoped that they were getting along better. Maybe Patti was just one of those kids who acted obnoxious because she was so afraid no one would like her. Maybe once she made some friends she'd be nicer.

I rounded the corner just in time to see Patti trip and fall into the pool. She came up for air, shrieking.

"Help, Dixie, help! I'm drowning!"

I ran to the pool and saw Patti going down quickly, sputtering and shrieking. For some crazy reason, the lifeguard's seat was empty.

Jodie stood there, her hand over her mouth. "Help her!" she cried.

I jumped into the pool.

THREE

She was going down again.

I dove down and managed to grab Patti under one arm, and using my free arm I swam with her to the edge of the pool. Her head lolled to one side. I couldn't tell if she was breathing.

A group gathered quickly. Bobby Babbit and Jimmy Lawrence, a C.I.T. from the blue team, lifted Patti out of the pool. Bobby quickly began to give Patti mouth-to-mouth resuscitation.

I pulled myself out of the pool and stood there dripping, praying that Patti would be all right.

"Breathe, Patti," I whispered out loud.

"I don't know what happened," Jodie wailed. "One second she was sitting next to me, the next she was in the pool!"

Finally, after what seemed like forever, Patti opened her eyes. She looked up at the faces surrounding her. I hurried over and knelt beside her. "Patti? Are you okay?"

"Wh-what happened?" she croaked out.

"You fell in, I guess," I said, stroking the wet hair off her forehead. "Don't you know how to swim?"

"A little," she managed. "But I guess I got scared or something."

"Do you think you can walk?" Bobby Babbit asked Patti.

She nodded yes, and he gently helped her up. "We'll just take you in to the nurse and let her get a look at you, okay?" He led her off into the country club.

Liza came running over, looking angrier than I'd ever seen her. "Who was supposed to be on lifeguard duty here?"

No one said a word.

She put her hands on her hips. "Look, a staff member is always on duty when the camp has use of the pools," Liza stated. "Someone might as well confess, because I can just go look it up."

Just at that moment, Dwayne Urlee, a senior counselor from the red team, came running over to us. I didn't know Dwayne very well. So far he hadn't been involved in any of the same activities as I had. There was something about him I didn't like, though. He always leered at girls when they walked by and made stupid sexist comments. Allie and Becky called him "Duh-Wayne."

"What happened?" Dwayne asked. "Why is everyone standing around the pool?"

Liza gave him a deadly look. "Were you on lifeguard duty?" she asked him.

"Yeah," he admitted. "I had to run to the john."

Liza walked right up to him and got in his face. "Don't you ever, *ever* leave a pool you are supposed to be guarding. Is that clear?"

"What am I supposed to do if nature calls?" Dwayne asked.

"Don't answer," Liza spit back at him. "A girl almost drowned just now. If she had, it would have been your fault."

The color drained out of Dwayne's face. "Yeah, okay. Sorry."

"Sorry doesn't cut it," Liza snapped at him. "If you slack off again, you're out of here."

"How's Patti?" Tori asked me at lunch.

Word about what had happened to Patti spread around the camp quickly. I had spent the entire morning with Patti, first just hanging out in the infirmary to make sure she was okay, then we took a slow walk around the camp grounds. Now we were at lunch, which was a buffet served outdoors near our campfire picnic area. Patti was in line with the other red team kids. I had decided to wait with my friends until the line got shorter.

"She seems fine," I told Tori, sitting down next to her on the redwood bench.

"I hear Duh-Wayne almost got canned for cutting out on his lifeguard duty," Becky said.

"I heard he told Liza he was in the john," Tori reported.

"I bet he was really busy leering at Dee Dee I've-got-it-so-I-flaunt-it De Witt," Allie guessed.

"So, is Patti okay now?" Becky asked. "What a horrible thing to have happen to the kid on her first day here, huh?"

"The strange thing is, I still don't see how it *did* happen," I said. "I mean, she was just standing there. And if she fell in, why couldn't she just grab the side?"

"I guess she got scared," Allie surmised. "She panicked."

"I guess," I agreed, pulling my knees up to my chest. "But it's weird. What's for lunch?"

"Barf on a bagel," Becky stated. "How can camp food be so bad when the country club food is so good? That's what I want to know."

"Different food service," I said. I looked at the full tray in the hands of a girl who was walking by. "It looks like egg salad."

"Hurl on a hoagie," Becky snorted.

"Lakeland to the rescue," Tori said. Out of the back pocket of her baggy shorts she pulled a huge chocolate bar. "Good thing it's not too hot today. It didn't melt," she reported, breaking off pieces for all of us.

"Hi. Can I sit with you?" Patti asked, walking over to us with her tray.

"Sure," I said, moving down the bench to make room for her. Her tray held two sandwiches, a mountain of potato chips spilling off the plate, and two pieces of chocolate cake.

"I guess your stomach is feeling better, huh?" Allie asked her.

"It will once I've eaten," Patti explained, biting into one of her sandwiches. She noticed us eating Tori's chocolate. "Where did you get that?"

"Tori," I said.

"Can I have some?" Patti asked.

"Nope," Tori said good-naturedly. "You have to eat the nutritional stuff."

"How come you don't?" Patti asked, taking another huge bite of egg salad.

"Because we are staff and you are a camper," Becky replied logically.

"No one here likes me," Patti stated, swallowing her food noisily. "Hey, is my tongue still pink?" she added, opening her mouth and sticking out her tongue with half-chewed egg salad on it.

"Oh please, no chew and show," Becky groaned.

"You have egg salad on your face," Allie pointed out.

Patti wiped her face with her napkin, then she propped her elbow in the dirty napkin to steady herself for another huge bite.

I was rapidly losing whatever appetite I had.

"Can I come over to your house after camp today?" Patti asked me, her mouth full.

"Uh, I'm sorry, no," I said, taken aback.

"Why?" Patti asked, stuffing down a handful of chips.

"I'm . . . busy," I told her.

"With what?" she asked me.

"Oh, you know, things," I said lamely.

She put her hand over her stomach. "This egg salad might be bad," she warned us. She gave me a sick look. "Can you come to the bathroom with me?"

"Why don't you run there, and I'll come along if you need me," I suggested.

Patti jumped up and ran for the bathroom. I buried my head in my hands. "I know it's wrong, y'all, but I just cannot stand that child!"

"I've never seen a kid quite like her before in my life," Allie marveled. "She's just so . . . so obnoxious!"

"Oh, she's okay," Tori said, breaking off some more chocolate and popping it into her mouth. "She's just scared."

"You like everybody," Becky told Tori.

Tori shrugged. "I'm still hungry. Want me to go grab some cake for everybody?"

"How can you eat after watching that girl ingest food?" I asked, feeling queasy.

"Oh, I can always eat," Tori said cheerfully, "as long as the food involved has no known nutritional value."

"Hello, worker ants," Dee Dee said as she sauntered by us, lapping at a giant chocolate chip cookie sandwich stuffed with chocolate ice cream.

"Where did you get that?" Tori asked her enviously.

"In the snack bar, where else?" Dee asked, taking another bite of her ice cream.

"But we're not allowed in the country club snack bar during camp," Allie protested.

"Well, I'm just *so* worried about getting caught," Dee Dee said sarcastically, licking the side of the cookie. Ethan walked by with another guy and Dee Dee watched him. "He's kind of cute, in a young sort of way. Who is he?"

"You'd hate him," Becky said quickly. "He's only thirteen."

"Yuck," Dee Dee said, making a face. "He might be fun to play with though."

"You talk so big," Becky jeered. "I'm not impressed."

"Really?" Dee Dee asked. "I'll have to ask your boyfriend, Ian, about that."

Becky's jaw hung open. "How do you know about my boyfriend?"

"Oh, my cousin Diana might have mentioned him when I called her. I told her I met you guys and she told me some very interesting information—such as that your boyfriend is the son of Graham Perry."

"How do you know it's her and not me?" Allie asked Dee Dee.

"Easy," Dee Dee replied. "Diana said Ian's girlfriend was the twin who had the big, ugly mole on her face." She took another bite of her ice cream sandwich. "Well, I might just have to call this Ian guy and introduce myself. I wouldn't mind hanging out at Graham Perry's house."

"He'll hate you," Becky spat at Dee Dee.

"You wish," Dee Dee taunted her, and then walked away.

Becky put her head in her hands. "I feel sick. I think I need some of Patti's pink stuff."

"Don't let Dee Dee get to you," I advised Becky. "Ian loves you. You told us so!"

"Yeah, that's right," Becky said, as if she were trying to talk herself into it. "But I've been so busy with camp and everything lately, I've hardly had a chance to see him."

A couple of picnic tables over, I saw Dee Dee stop to talk with Ethan. I got a sinking feeling when I saw the two of them laughing together.

And then a brilliant idea hit me.

"Y'all, I have a great idea," I said slowly.

"We kill Dee Dee before she steals all our boyfriends?" Becky asked.

"Much better," I replied. "My aunt and uncle are planning this big barbecue on Sunday. It's for everyone in the area who was in *Sunset Beach Slaughter,* the last movie they wrote." My aunt and uncle write horror movies, and their last movie had been filmed right on Sunset Island. Carrie Alden, the au pair who worked for rock star Graham Perry's family, actually had a part in it.

"Okay, so they're having a barbecue at the haunted house," Allie said, referring to the huge old house where my cousin Molly lives with her parents and her friend Darcy, and where I was living for the summer. "What does that have to do with us?"

"Well, I was thinking," I continued. "I'm sure it would be okay if I invited y'all. And Becky, you could invite Ian. And I could invite Ethan." I turned to Tori. "And you could invite Tim!"

"But what about him having the flu?" Tori asked.

"Well, I'll bet he'll be better by Sunday," I pointed out.

"And I could invite Pete Tilly!" Allie exclaimed. "I love it!"

"It'll be so much fun!" I cried. "And we'll get to spend time with the boys we like, which will make it much harder for Dee Dee to move in on them. Don't you think?"

"You are kind of brilliant in your own sweet, Southern way," Becky said with a grin.

"Great plan for you guys," Tori said, "but I could never call Tim and invite him."

"Sure you could!" Allie insisted.

"Not, not, never, never, unh-uh," Tori protested. "Forget it. My throat would close up. Or else something totally dumb will come out of my mouth. Or I'll belch right into the phone—yeah, that's what will happen—and then he'll—"

"We'll help you," Allie interrupted. "You can practice on us before you call him."

"Greetings, Earthlings," Jodie said, strolling over to us. She put one foot up on the picnic bench. "Hey, I was just in the ladies' room, and that dweeby new girl is in there heaving."

"Oh no!" I exclaimed. I had forgotten all about her.

"Oh yes," Jodie insisted. "It's majorly disgusting. She keeps yelling for you between heaves, in case you care."

I jumped up from the picnic table.

"Hey, better take her pink stuff," Becky reminded me, handing me the little purse Patti had left at our table.

I grabbed the purse and ran.

FOUR

"Are you sure I can't come over?" Patti asked me, desperately clutching my hand.

It was the end of the camp day. The last bus sat there idling, waiting for Patti to get on it.

"Sorry, honey," I replied. "Maybe another time."

"Tomorrow we'll do everything together, okay?" she said anxiously.

"Let's go!" the bus driver called to Patti. "Everyone is waiting on you!"

"Bye-bye!" I said gaily, ignoring her comment and waving as she got on the bus. "See you tomorrow!"

As the bus drove off, I turned to my friends. "Help! I'm going to kill her! I can't take one more day of her! I can't live through a whole entire summer of her!"

"She must hate it at home to be that desperate," Tori said, shaking her head. "Anyway, she'll get better once she gets to know other kids."

"No, no, she won't!" I insisted hysterically. "She's glommed on to me like some kind of horrid fungus!"

Becky laughed. "Now, now, Dix," she chided me, "remember how you're a Southern lady and everything."

"Yeah, watch it or your tiara will slip," Allie teased.

"Y'all, this is no joke!" I cried.

"Hey, Dixie, this message just came in for you at the office," Jimmy Lawrence, a C.I.T. for the blue team, said, walking over to us and handing me a note. He turned to Tori. "Hi," he mumbled, staring at the grass.

"Hi," she mumbled back.

Silence.

"So, see ya," he finally said.

"Yeah, see ya," Tori managed to reply.

Becky nudged Tori. "Jimmy Lawrence likes you."

"That's just because he's the only one at camp shyer than me," Tori said. She pulled a piece of red licorice out of her pocket and stuck it in her mouth.

"Molly just called," I told my friends after scanning the note. "Her van broke down and she wants to know if I can get a ride home."

"Yeah, sure," Becky said. "Sam's coming for us and we're taking Tori. But it's a big car."

"Speak of the devil," Allie said, cocking her head toward the red Cadillac convertible that was heading toward us.

"Nice car," I said.

"Dad just got it," Becky informed me. "I think Kiki talked him into it."

Kiki Coors was an actress who Becky and Allie had hired to pretend to be their mom for Parents' Day at camp. Now she was actually dating their father.

"So they're still dating," I commented.

"Dating isn't exactly the word I'd use," Allie sniffed. "What's it called when the person is, like, a permanent fixture in your house?"

"They're *living* together?" I asked, aghast.

"No," Becky admitted. "But she's over at our house just about every day. Or else he's over at her place in Portland."

"Hi!" Sam called as she pulled up in the car. "Hey, are these wheels fine or what?"

"The red car clashes with your red hair," Allie pointed out.

"So we'll bleach the car," Sam replied.

I laughed. Sam is really wonderful and funny. And she is so terrific looking. She was wearing cut-offs, a denim bra top with peace symbols all over it, and her trademark red cowboy boots.

"Can we give Dixie a ride home?" Becky asked.

"Sure thing," Sam said. "Hop in."

Sam pulled around the private drive and down the street from the country club. Then she pulled out on to Beach Avenue. "So, how's life in the fast lane?" she asked us.

"We met the camper from hell today," Becky reported.

"Oh, forget about camp!" Allie cried. "We're free! Crank up the tunes!"

"You got it," Sam said, and she pushed a cassette into the tape deck.

"You're a love junkie, a love junkie baby!" a male voice wailed.

"Great song," I yelled over the music. "Who is that?"

"My band," Sam said proudly, "the Flirts."

Tori leaned forward from the backseat. "You guys are great!" she yelled. "I heard you play a couple of times at the Play Café!"

"Wow, you actually have your own band?" I asked Sam, truly impressed.

"So?" Becky said. "We have our own band, too. It's no big deal."

"Your band makes noise. My band makes music," Sam pointed out.

"You mean y'all have a record out and everything?" I asked Sam.

"Not yet," she admitted. "What you're listening to is just a demo—demonstration tape. We almost had a deal with Polimar Records—It's a long story."

"We almost had a deal, too," Becky reminded Sam.

"Whatever," Sam said, looking over her shoulder before pulling into the left-hand lane and turning the car toward Hangman's Hill, at the top of which is my cousin's house.

"You really *live* up there?" Tori asked as Sam

turned the car up the hill. Tori hadn't been over to the house yet.

"You must know about this house," I said. "You've lived on this island all your life."

"Well, yeah," Tori agreed. "But I didn't realize you meant *that* house." She gazed up at the house as the car climbed the steep hill. "That house is haunted. Every kid on the island knows that."

"I certainly hope it's haunted," I said seriously. "My cousin's family would be so disappointed if it weren't." My aunt and uncle are a little . . . how can I put it . . . strange. Not only do they write horror movies, they kind of live their lives like they're in the middle of one. It's really very funny when you think about the fact that my parents are the most conservative people in the world. I mean, how did my uncle and my father, who are brothers, turn out so totally different?

The house is this huge old Victorian thing, with massive shutters and an oversized door with a knocker in the shape of a skull. Inside there are permanent bloody handprints on the guest towels, and there's a fruit bowl with a plastic bloody hand in it. The back doorbell doesn't ring, it lets out a blood-curdling scream. My uncle and aunt always dress in black and their butler—they really and truly have a butler—is tall and skinny and models himself after Lurch, from

43

the Addams Family. Meanwhile my uncle goes by the name Gomez.

There is absolutely nothing about a family like this in my mother's book, *The Happy Homemaker*.

Which is exactly why I love the Masons so much.

"Y'all want to come in?" I asked as Sam pulled the car up in front of the house.

Just then Darcy Laken stuck her head out. She is nineteen and is Molly's best friend. She lives with the Masons and helps care for Molly. She's also friends with Sam and Sam's two best friends, Emma Cresswell and Carrie Alden. I think that Darcy is just the coolest. She's tall and athletic and has the most beautiful long dark hair. She told me very matter-of-factly that her family is kind of poor and my aunt and uncle are helping her go to college. She's very direct—something I don't see a lot of in the South.

"Yo, Bridges!" she called to Sam. "Come on in and take a load off!"

Sam turned off the car. "How do you like the wheels?" she asked Darcy as she jumped out of the car. We all piled out, too.

"Great," Darcy replied. She turned to Molly, who wheeled herself up next to Darcy. "Check out Sam's car."

"Hot," Molly commented.

My cousin Molly is darling, with wavy brown hair and a pretty face. When she's not in her wheelchair you can't really tell she's paralyzed from the waist down. But I feel so awful. Sometimes I have terrible dreams about it, as if it's me in that car accident, and me who can never walk again. I would never tell Molly. How could I compare my nightmares with her reality?

"When did you get it?" Molly asked Sam.

"It's Mr. Jacobs's," Sam admitted. "I only wish it was mine. By the time I can afford a car like this I'll be too old to appreciate it."

"Come on in," Molly urged us.

"And live to tell the tale?" Tori whispered to me as she carefully walked into the cavernous front hall. She looked all around. Still photos from various horror movies had been blown up to poster size and hung on the walls.

"Refreshments?" Lurch asked in his low growl, coming up behind us.

"Eek!" Tori screamed, and jumped up about a foot.

I laughed. "Lurch, this is Tori. Tori, Lurch. You know everyone else."

"Lurch?" Tori repeated, and gulped hard.

Lurch descended on her. "Do you have a problem with my naaaaaame?"

"No, no, oh, not at all!" Tori insisted, jumping backward. "I love your name! Yep! It's a keen name all right!"

Lurch growled and went into the kitchen.

Tori looked like she was going to faint, and the rest of us laughed.

"It's a joke!" Becky explained. "His real name is Simon. He used to be an actor in horror movies, but he retired."

"We just about lost it the first time we ever came here with Sam, too," Allie added. "It was for a party earlier this summer. We freaked out!"

"People don't actually, like, *die* here, right?" Tori asked nervously.

"Only if we really don't like them," Molly replied offhandedly.

"We hang the bodies in a meat freezer in the cellar," Darcy added brightly. "Come on, I'll show ya!"

"Oh, I'll just take your word for it," Tori said quickly, pulling away from Darcy. Her eyes kept shifting around the room. "And I thought being raised by hippie parents was bizarre."

Molly laughed. "Let's go hang out in the kitchen," she suggested, wheeling her chair down the hall. "Darcy and I baked some killer chocolate chip cookies."

We all sat around the huge table, where Lurch had left us some lemonade and glasses.

"This stuff isn't poisoned or anything, right?" Tori asked, picking up a glass of lemonade.

"You're just a big old baby," I teased Tori, reaching for a cookie. I turned to my cousin. "I was wondering,

Molly, would it be okay if a few of my friends and their boyfriends came to the barbecue on Sunday?"

"Sure," Molly said with a shrug. "You know how my parents are—the more the merrier."

"Hey, I don't have a boyfriend," Tori put in. "You can't call Tim my boyfriend."

"Would you like him to be your boyfriend?" Darcy asked her.

"Well, yeah," Tori admitted, reaching for her second cookie. "But it'll never happen."

"Bad attitude," Sam stated. "Mmm, these cookies are killer."

"How can I have a good attitude?" Tori asked plaintively. "Boys make me crazy! I turn into a total dweeb around them!"

"They're just people," Molly said with a shrug.

"No, they're not!" Tori insisted. "They're boys!"

Molly turned to me. "So, who's your boyfriend, cuz?" she asked.

"Well, I guess he's not really my boyfriend," I confessed shyly. "Yet!"

"That-a-girl!" Sam cheered.

"His name is Ethan Hewitt," I said, enjoying the sound of his name on my lips.

Sam practically spewed her lemonade. "Ethan Hewitt? The kid Emma babysits for?"

"Emma babysits for Ethan's little brother and sister, for your information," Becky said heatedly.

"And he happens to be thirteen," Allie added.

"Okay, okay, I'm sorry," Sam managed. "I'm just not used to thinking of him as heartbreak material."

"But he's so darling!" I exclaimed. "And so sweet!" I put my chin in my hands. "Don't you think he looks kind of like a cute young movie star?"

"Not the last time I saw him," Sam said, stretching her long legs out in front of her.

Becky kicked her under the table.

"Okay, sorry, he's probably grown up a lot and I just didn't notice," Sam added hastily.

"He has," Allie said with dignity. "You think just because a guy is young he can't be cute, and you're wrong."

"You and Emma are coming to the barbecue with Carrie, aren't you?" Darcy asked Sam.

"Yeah, we'll be there," Sam said. "We're gonna bring our guys, if that's okay."

"Oh, sure," Darcy said.

"Uh, excuse me," Tori murmured in a low voice. "But there's something red and gunky and disgusting in the bottom of this glass of lemonade."

Molly peered into Tori's glass. "Oh," she said. "That's blood."

Tori gulped hard. "You're kidding I hope."

"Why would I do a thing like that?" Molly asked innocently.

"Y'all, quit picking on Tori," I chided them. "It's a

maraschino cherry and cherry juice," I told Tori. "It's Lurch's idea of a joke. He did the same thing to me the first day I came here."

Tori attempted a laugh. "Really funny. Wow, what a prankster!"

"Oh yeah, he's a ton of laughs," Darcy agreed. "Just wait till you see what he barbecues on Sunday!"

FIVE

These are my mother's favorite words: "Be sweet."

Now I believe in being sweet. I really do. But by the end of that week it was becoming completely impossible to "be sweet" to Patti Chernick.

She followed me everywhere. She held my hand. She told everyone I was her "very best friend in the whole world." She had two more episodes of stomach upheaval and the only thing that would help was for me to be with her, holding a damp cloth to her forehead while she lost her cookies.

Now is that disgusting, or what?

Patti was right about one thing she'd said that very first day of camp: kids hated her. And things did not get any better as the week progressed. If anything, they got worse. Campers took to calling her "Pink Stuff" instead of Patti, after that awful stomach medicine she carried around. Some particularly nasty boys called her "Porky Pink Stuff." Liza had a serious talk with them about kindness, which simply led them to do it behind Patti's back instead of to her face.

As for me, I tried to like her. I tried to concentrate on her good qualities. I tried to "be sweet" until the cows came home. But she'd gaze at me with those big old eyes of hers, clutch my fingers in her sweaty hand, and constantly ask to be with me. She followed me everywhere. She bragged about herself, and on top of that she had no sense of humor. Although I felt sorry for her and I hated that kids were cruel to her, the truth of the matter was: I was ready to kill the child.

I didn't let on, though. I couldn't. I was her only friend.

"What are you doing this weekend?" Patti asked me on Friday, as we put away the paints from an arts and crafts project. Everyone else was out playing volley-ball. Patti stayed behind to be with me, per usual.

"Oh, nothing special," I replied, looking around for the top to the red poster paint.

"Can I come over?" she asked me, as she did every day.

"Oh, I don't think so, Patti," I replied. "I'm busy."

"Doing what?"

"Things." I found the top to the paint and screwed it on.

"What things?" Patti demanded.

"Why don't you clean up that paper and throw it in the trash?" I suggested to her, eager to change the subject.

She dutifully went over to the table and began to

gather up the leftover paper. "A little birdie told me you were having a party Sunday," Patti said slyly.

"Who told you that?"

"Someone," she said evasively.

"Well, honey, it's not my party. It's my aunt and uncle's party, for a movie they wrote," I explained.

"Am I invited?" she asked me hopefully.

"Sorry," I told her gently.

"Does that mean I'm not invited?" she pressed.

It was at moments like this that I wanted to kill her most.

"Patti, it's not polite to ask someone to invite you somewhere," I said. "Besides, I can't really invite campers to the party. It wouldn't be fair."

"I know," she sighed. She grabbed a paintbrush matted with blue paint and swished it over the table toward me. "It's because I'm fat, isn't it?"

"No!" I exclaimed. "Of course not! And you're not really fat, you're . . . plump."

"Okay, then, it's because I'm ugly," Patti said matter-of-factly.

"Oh, no, it's not!" I insisted. "You are not ugly at all!"

"My father says I am," she replied. "He says I'm fat and ugly, and that's why no one wants to be with me."

I stopped cleaning up and sat down. "Does he really say that?"

She nodded.

I went to her and put my arms around her. "Oh

Patti, it isn't true," I told her. "I'm really sorry that he says things like that to you."

"He hates me," she said with a shrug, as she reached for the paintbrush and began to make circles on the table.

"We're supposed to be cleaning up, not painting on the tables," I reminded her.

She went and got a sponge and cleaned off the table. "Want to know what I wish?" she asked in a low voice.

"What?"

She looked at me, her eyes huge in her pale moon face. "I wish I was you."

"Thank you, Patti. But being you can be wonderful," I assured her.

"Why?" she asked me.

"Well, because . . . you're smart. And, and . . ." I tried desperately to think of something else nice to say about her. "From what I've heard you're a really good singer!" What I didn't add was that I'd "heard" this from Patti herself.

"That's true," she agreed. "So, do you like me?"

"Be sweet" echoed in my head. "Of course I like you," I lied.

"Good, then we can do everything together—forever," Patti said happily, grabbing my hand.

We headed out to the volleyball court. Tori was

captain of the red team, and she was serving the ball. Allie and Becky were both in the back line.

"Wouldn't you like to play the next game?" I asked Patti.

"No, I hate sports," she said. "I'd rather stay here with you."

The littlest kids on the red team were standing together, holding the pom-poms we'd made in arts and crafts.

"Hey, Dixie, listen to this!" Shyla, a darling six-year-old African-American girl yelled to me from the other side of the volleyball court. She turned to her friends. "Okay? Ready!"

> Swing to the left,
> Swing to the right.
> Red team, red team,
> Fight, fight, fight!
> Yeeahhhhh!!

They all jumped up and down and shook their pom-poms. I got my hand loose from Patti's and applauded them. They were doing one of the cheers I had taught them the day before.

"That was so fabulous!" I called over to them.

"Cheerleading is stupid," Patti said.

"Hi," Ethan said, walking over to me. "Your team is winning."

55

"Great!" I exclaimed.

Ethan pushed the hair out of his eyes. "It's because of Tori. She's a really terrific athlete."

"Sports are stupid," Patti said.

Ethan ignored her. "So, about Sunday, I thought I'd just get a ride over with Emma—she's my brother and sister's au pair—she's invited, too."

I nodded. "Darcy told me Emma, Carrie, and Sam are all coming."

"So, we should be there at three, right?" Ethan asked.

"Yep," I replied.

"Cool," Ethan said. "I can't wait to see this haunted house you live in. Emma keeps telling me about it."

I laughed. "You kind of have to see it for yourself to believe it."

We watched the game for a few minutes. The blue team lost the ball to the red team.

"I better go back to my team," Ethan said. "Catch ya later."

Patti narrowed her eyes at me. "How come he's coming to your house and I can't come?"

I wanted to scream. "He's my date," I explained. "And you're not."

"Want to join the red team, Patti?" Liza asked, walking over to us.

"No," Patti said. "Volleyball is stupid."

"They ought to use Porky Pink Stuff for the balls," a boy with braces snorted loudly to his friend.

Patti didn't say a word. She just reached for my hand and held it tight.

I managed to sneak a look at my watch. Only an hour left and camp would be out for the week. And I could spend two whole days without Patti Chernick.

I stared at my reflection in the mirror, hoping I looked okay. It was Sunday afternoon and the guests were due to arrive any minute.

I was so excited—it was the very first date of my entire life. With a boy. A cute boy. My parents would just kill me if they knew.

I twirled around, hoping I was dressed okay. I had on a sheer pink and white baby-doll top over white shorts.

"Dixie!" Darcy called to me from downstairs. "Your friends are here. They're coming up."

Allie, Becky, and Tori filed into my room.

"Oh, y'all look so darling!" I exclaimed.

Allie had on a man's vest and jeans with holes in them over white lace tights. Becky had on cutoffs, a short-sleeved red sweater that bared her midriff and combat boots. And Tori had on hot pink overalls over a stretchy baby T-shirt, with high-top pink sneakers on her feet.

"Who cares if I look good?" Tori lamented, falling onto my bed. "I got a call from Tim right before I left the house and his parents won't let him out. They said he's not over the flu."

"Oh, that's awful," I sympathized. "Are the other guys coming?"

"Ian is for sure," Becky said confidently. She stared at herself in the mirror over my dresser. "I'm getting a major zit."

"Ethan, too," I added, looking at her reflection. "I don't see a zit."

"Well, Pete said maybe," Allie reported. "I don't know what that means."

"Oh, who cares about stupid guys, anyway?" Tori asked. She popped up from the bed. "Now I can just have a good time and not have to worry."

Molly wheeled herself into the doorway. "You guys coming downstairs?"

"In just a sec," I told her.

"See you down there," she replied and headed for the small elevator down the hall.

"Does she have a boyfriend?" Tori wondered aloud.

"She's kind of seeing Howie Lawrence," I said. "You know, Jimmy's older brother."

"Would you go out with a guy in a wheelchair?" Tori asked me.

"Sure, if I really liked him." I took one last look at myself in the mirror. "Would you?"

"I'm not the right person to ask," Tori replied, "since I'm never going to have a date in my entire life."

"I really am getting a zit," Becky insisted, now peering into a hand mirror from her purse. "Right on my chin. A crater. I can feel it."

"There's some zit stuff in the medicine cabinet in the bathroom," I told her.

She went into my bathroom and got the tube. "Oh, hey, Allie and I have an idea," she called from the bathroom. "Since we have to be at camp so early Tuesday morning for this stupid white-water rafting trip, what about if you guys stay over at our house tomorrow night? Then Sam can drive us to camp."

"Sounds like fun," Tori agreed, idly looking through a book on astronomy near my bed.

"I'd love to," I added happily.

"Do you really read this stuff for fun?" Tori asked me.

"Sure," I said. "What do you read for fun?"

"I don't," Tori said. "I can't sit still that long." As if to illustrate her point, she jumped up. "Let's go!"

Downstairs the party was already in full swing. Allie and Tori took off for the Frisbee game out on the lawn. I scanned the crowd. About fifty or so people milled about. Some looked like they were right out of a horror movie—black clothes, white face makeup, monster masks, the works. Others looked like perfectly normal teenagers—a bunch of them had been extras in *Sunset Beach Slaughter.* Lurch stood behind a portable bar serving drinks. I noticed Sam was standing near the table of food with a gorgeous guy with a ponytail.

"Is that Sam's boyfriend?" I asked Becky.

"Yeah, is he to die for, or what?" Becky replied. "His name is Pres Travis. He's the bass player for Flirting With Danger—the Flirts, you know."

"He looks like a movie star," I whispered.

"Come on, I'll introduce you."

She dragged me over to Sam and the group she was standing with. "This is Pres Travis," Becky said, "And that's Emma Cresswell, Carrie Alden, and Billy Sampson. And this is Molly's cousin, Dixie Mason."

"Nice to meet you," I said with a grin.

"Hey, this is unreal!" Sam exclaimed, looking from Emma to me and back to Emma again. "This kid could be your little sister. I swear to God!"

Everyone turned to look at me.

"You're right," Carrie agreed. She smiled at me. "You're like a junior Emma!"

Now, this was a wonderful compliment, as far as I was concerned. Because Emma Cresswell was just gorgeous.

"I don't have a little sister and I've always wanted one," Emma said. "So that's very nice."

Billy put his arm around Carrie and sipped from the can of Coke he was holding. "So, how are you liking Sunset Island?"

"Oh, I just love it to death!" I cried.

He laughed. "Whoa, great accent! Where are you from?"

"Mississippi," I replied. "Where I come from we think y'all have accents!" I turned to Carrie. She was cute in a really natural way. "I heard you were in the last movie my aunt and uncle made."

"Don't remind me," Carrie said with a groan. "I don't think it even made it into any first-run movie theaters it was so awful."

"But they live for awful movies!" I exclaimed. "It's their claim to fame! Who did you play?"

"A waitress who got hacked to death," Carrie admitted.

"She was a thing of beauty, too," Pres drawled, with a Tennessee accent, wrapping an arm around Sam's waist.

"Now, there's a guy without an accent!" I said.

Everyone laughed.

"Hi," Ethan said, coming up beside me. "Darcy just gave me a tour of the place. It's awesome!"

"Hi," I said. Suddenly I felt kind of shy. It was so weird. I mean I had been standing there laughing it up with eighteen and nineteen year olds, but now that Ethan was standing there, I felt self-conscious.

It really was a date. Me. On a date. I had dreamt about what it would be like, and now it was actually happening. My parents' faces flew into my head, both of them looking so stern and disapproving that I heard myself gasp. Then I felt my throat close up a little, which is a feeling I get sometimes right before I have an asthma attack. I felt for the inhaler in my back pocket, just in case.

But no. I couldn't possibly have an asthma attack. It would be too embarrassing. I wasn't doing anything wrong. I was just at a party with a boy, like any other normal girl. I closed my eyes for a quick second, willing away my parents' angry faces, willing myself to breathe normally.

"You okay?" Ethan asked me.

Everyone was staring at us.

"Oh, sure, I'm fine," I assured him. "Want to go for a walk?"

"Sure," he said casually.

"Have fun," Sam called to us.

We walked away from the crowd, down the path that led to the woods in back of the house.

"So, your relatives are really strange, huh?" Ethan said.

"In a wonderful kind of way," I added.

"Oh, yeah, I agree!" Ethan said enthusiastically. "My parents are just lawyers. I mean, they're totally normal."

We started downhill and my foot slipped. Ethan grabbed my hand. And he didn't let go. We were holding hands.

Yes! Yes! Yes! I pretended it was no big thing.

"So, camp's pretty fun, huh?" Ethan said.

"I like it."

"I wish I never had to go back to school in the fall," Ethan said. "I mean, I get good grades and all that—"

"Me too," I agreed.

"But it's so boring," he continued. "I feel like even the teachers are bored."

"Some of my teachers are like that," I said, stepping over a small boulder in the path. "But some of them are good. I have this great science teacher, Mrs. Goldman. She has a high-powered telescope in her backyard, and she lets us come over and use it."

"You interested in outer space?" Ethan wondered.

"Oh, I love it," I said passionately. "It's like a big mystery, you know? Someday I'm going to walk in space."

"That would be awesome," Ethan agreed. "You should do it."

I looked at him out of the corner of my eye. "You aren't going to crack any jokes about it? That's what boys usually do."

"Heck no," Ethan said, still holding tightly to my hand. "You're really smart. You should do whatever you want to do."

I grinned at him. "I knew you were wonderful."

Ethan's face turned bright red, but he looked happy, too. I just kept grinning. I couldn't stop! I felt too wonderful!

"Hey, I'm starving. Want to go back and get some barbecue?" I asked him.

"As long as they don't serve it all bloody," Ethan said with a shudder. "I heard this house is full of practical horror jokes."

We turned around to head back up the hill. "Well, it might be safer to be a vegetarian," I said with a laugh.

We climbed until we came to the top of the path leading to the house. Ethan was still holding my hand, which meant that soon everyone would see him holding my hand, which as far as I was concerned meant we would officially be "A Couple."

Everything was just so terrific. Nothing could possibly go wrong.

"Dixie! Dixie! Dixie!"

A round figure came running across the huge lawn toward us.

I recognized that run. But it couldn't be.

The figure tripped, fell, and got up again.

My mind screamed no, no, no, but my eyes told me yes, yes, yes.

It was Patti Chernick.

SIX

"I cannot believe that Patti Chernick just showed up at your house yesterday," Allie said.

It was after camp the next day, and we were riding back to Allie and Becky's house in the red convertible, Sam at the wheel.

"Don't remind me," I groaned. "She followed me and Ethan everywhere."

"You guys didn't get to be alone at all?" Tori asked me.

"Not after she showed up," I said mournfully.

"What nerve!" Becky exclaimed.

"Didn't you invite that kid?" Sam asked, looking at me through the rearview mirror.

"No, I didn't. In fact, I specifically told her she was not invited," I explained. "But she told her parents that she was invited as my special guest, so they just dropped her off! Then I had no way to get rid of her until they came to pick her up two hours later!"

"Can you imagine how miserable and lonely she must be?" Tori mused.

A guilty stab clutched at my stomach. "Do you think I was too mean to her?" I asked my friends. "Do you think that's why she wasn't at camp today?"

"Too mean?" Allie repeated. "Dixie, get a grip! You're a saint with that kid!"

"Besides, Liza said Patti's mom called and said Patti wasn't feeling well," Becky reminded me. "Her not being at camp doesn't have anything to do with you."

"What is wrong with that kid's stomach? That's what I want to know." Tori shuddered. "It is seriously gross—she spends her life looking down a porcelain bowl!"

"Is she bulemic or something?" Sam asked. "I mean, is she making herself barf? I noticed she got sick at the barbecue yesterday."

"I asked Liza about it," Allie said. "Liza talked with Patti's mom. Patti's mom said that Patti has a 'delicate stomach.'"

"Oh, give me a major break!" Becky exclaimed. "Does that mean that Dixie should spend the rest of the summer locked up with that kid in the girls' john while she shows off her inner beauty?"

Everyone in the car cracked up at that except me. I was picturing myself day after day after day, holding on to Patti's clammy hand while she unloaded her "delicate stomach."

"Sam, what would you do?" I asked plaintively,

scooching forward in the seat so she could hear me. "I don't want to be mean to Patti, but she won't leave me alone!"

"Maybe you could try to find her a friend her own age," Sam suggested, as she stopped the car at a red light.

"Fat chance," Becky snorted. "Other kids hate her because she's obnoxious! They call her names!"

"Well, maybe you need to level with her then," Sam said.

"What am I supposed to say?" I queried. "No offense, Patti, but no one likes you because you're real obnoxious?"

"Well, maybe not quite like that," Sam said. "But the kid is responsible for her own behavior, you know. You're not doing her any favors by pretending she's acting normal."

I threw myself back on the seat. "I could never say anything to her," I said with a sigh. "I just couldn't."

Sam pulled the car into the Jacobses' driveway and turned off the ignition. "Hey, what time do you guys have to be at camp in the morning for this rafting thing?" she asked us.

"Six o'clock," Becky reported glumly, as we all piled out of the car.

Sam put her hands on her hips. "Hold the phone. I'm supposed to be awake to drive you to camp at, like, five forty-five *in the morning*?"

"You can go back to sleep," Becky pointed out, "whereas we have to go break our necks on some stupid rafts."

"It's gonna be fun!" Allie exclaimed.

"Thank you so much, Ranger Rick," Becky snapped at her sister.

"Hey, can we get a snack?" Tori asked. "I'm starved."

"A girl after my own heart," Sam said with a laugh. "I'm always starved myself. How about some leftover pizza and chocolate brownies?"

"With sausage and pepperoni on the pizza and lots of white sugar in the brownies I hope," Tori rhapsodized. "Yum! All the things my parents think are poison! I'm in!"

"Dumb movie," Tori said, as the credits rolled across the TV.

It was later that night and we had rented one of the Masons' horror movies, *Nerds With Knives,* and we were stuffing ourselves with popcorn, fried chicken, and jelly beans all through it. Allie and Becky's dad, Dan Jacobs, and his new girlfriend, Kiki Coors, sat on the couch cuddling. Sam was out with Emma and Carrie at the Play Café.

"I thought the scene where the nerds attacked the surfer dudes on the beach was pretty funny," Becky said. She stretched and turned to me. "Anyhow, next

68

time your aunt and uncle do a teen horror movie, you've just got to get me a part in it."

"How come you weren't in *Sunset Beach Slaughter*?" I asked her, fishing the last few jellybeans out of the bowl.

"Oh, they said we were too young," Becky explained, rolling her eyes.

"Well, honey, you are too young," Kiki agreed.

Dan Jacobs smiled at his girlfriend. "I guess you'd be just about the right age though, right?"

Kiki grinned back at him. "Well, that thought did occur to me," she admitted. She looked over at me. "I'd really appreciate it if you'd give my picture and resume to your aunt and uncle."

"Please," Allie snorted, giving Kiki a look of disgust. "These are *teen* horror films. The operative word here is '*teen*.'"

"But Kiki could play, say, the young and gorgeous teacher of the teens, something like that," Dan suggested.

"Gag me," Becky mumbled.

Kiki looked at her watch. "Well, it's pretty late. And I know that you kids have to get up really early for your rafting trip, so you might want to hit the hay."

"Excuse me," Allie said. "But who died and made you boss?"

Mr. Jacobs flushed. "Allie, you will not talk to any adult like that in this house."

"Dad!" Allie exclaimed. "We hired her to pretend to be our mother, and now she thinks she really is!"

"I'm sorry if that's how it sounded," Kiki said. "It was just a suggestion, because I care about you guys."

Becky and Allie gave each other a look that said they didn't believe that about Kiki for one second.

"Come on," Becky said. "Let's go up to our room where we can have some privacy."

"Night," Tori said cheerfully to Mr. Jacobs. "Thanks for the hospitality and everything."

"Thanks for letting us stay over," I added. Tori and I carried the empty food bowls into the kitchen and put them in the dishwasher. Then we hustled upstairs to join the twins.

Becky put a Graham Perry tape into her tape player and plopped down on the bed. "I really cannot stand Kiki," she said.

"I think she's nice," Tori said, reaching for the copy of *Teen World* magazine that was on the dresser.

"Is there anyone you don't like?" Allie asked Tori grouchily.

Tori thought about it a minute. "Not really."

"Not even Dee Dee De Witt?" Allie pressed.

"Nah," Tori said. "It's a waste of energy." She looked closer at the fashion spread in the magazine. "Wow, this stuff is seriously warped. Who's gonna wear see-through clothes with a see-through bra?"

"Dee Dee De Witt!" Becky and Allie yelled in unison.

I unrolled my sleeping bag and sat down on it cross-legged. "Y'all, I cannot believe that Dee Dee is coming on this raft trip tomorrow."

"She had to, probably," Tori said, plopping herself down on Becky's bed. "Liza said all the red team counselors have to go."

Becky opened some pink nail polish and began to apply it to her fingernails. "Oh, you guys didn't hear the worst of it," she told us. "Liza put Dee Dee and Pete in charge of deciding who goes on which raft!"

"No way!" I exclaimed.

"Yes way," Becky replied. "Dee Dee is supposed to know all about white-water rafting—she did it in the Alps or something like that. And according to Liza she's a qualified lifeguard and she's been in professional water ballets in Europe."

"Dee Dee De Witt?" I asked incredulously. "I can't believe she's ever lifted a finger in her life unless it was to reel some boy in!"

"You can't judge a book by looking at the cover," Tori singsonged.

"I've already seen more than her cover, thank you very much," Becky said, undoing the French braid in her hair.

"Did you see her with Pete Tilly today?" Allie asked. "She was totally all over him! It was gross!"

"And she's after Ethan, too," Becky added grimly. "She was, like, breathing in his ear at the pool!"

"Every time she saw me she'd get this triumphant look on her face," I added with a sigh.

"Hey, you have to hate her," Allie told Tori. "You're our best friend, and she's our enemy."

"The way I see it is this," Tori explained, putting her hands behind her head. "It's like this karma thing. If Dee Dee De Witt is awful in this lifetime, she's gonna come back as a cockroach or something."

I pulled off my sneakers. "You mean you believe in reincarnation?"

"Maybe," Tori said with a shrug. "It kind of makes sense to me."

"But don't you believe in heaven and hell?" I wondered.

"Nah," Tori said. "Too depressing."

I stared at Tori in awe. I didn't know anyone who didn't believe in heaven and hell. Heaven and hell are very big in my family.

"I read this really cool book about people who had near-death experiences," Allie said excitedly, turning over onto her stomach. "They all said they saw a white light and they felt really peaceful. And then some dead relative told them it wasn't time for them to die yet, so they came back into their earthly body."

Becky shuddered. "It sounds like one of the Masons' horror movies." She held out her hand and scrutinized the nail polish. "Is this too pink?"

Allie looked over at her sister's fingers. "Yeah. It's kind of Patti Chernick pink-stuff pink, isn't it?"

"Listen y'all," I began meaningfully. "You have to help me out on this trip tomorrow. If Patti stays glued to me, please, please, please, just try to get her away from me for a little while so I can be alone with Ethan!"

"We'll try," Tori agreed, "but the kid lives for you and you alone. I doubt we can unglue her from your side."

"Oh, just great," I moaned. "That means that I'll spend the trip with Patti and Dee Dee will spend the trip with Ethan!"

"We'll figure something out," Becky promised, wiping the nail polish off her left hand with a cotton ball. "We can't let Dee Dee get away with that."

"Why are you taking off the polish?" Tori asked.

"It really does look too much like the pink stuff," Becky said, making a face.

There was a soft knock on the door.

"Yeah?" Becky called.

Sam stuck her head in. "Hi, did you guys have fun?"

"Come on in," I said eagerly—I love being around Sam.

"We watched a horror movie and ate a lot of junk,"

Allie reported. "Becky tried to call Ian, but he wasn't home. What did you do?"

"Hung out at the Play Café with Emma and Carrie," Sam said, sitting on the edge of Becky's bed. "Diana De Witt showed up in this practically see-through shirt—serious overkill. Her little cousin was with her—the one you guys told me about."

"Dee Dee De Witt," I groaned.

"Senior poison and junior poison," Sam shuddered, "that's what they look like to me. Mondo bad news." She got up from Becky's bed. "Well, I just wanted to say hi. Have fun, you guys."

"Sam," I asked, stopping her as she was on her way out the door. "If a boy really, truly likes you, do you think it's possible for another girl to get him away from you just by being a big flirt?"

She leaned against the door frame. "Are you talking about Dee Dee De Witt and Ethan Hewitt or are you talking theoretical?"

"Dee Dee and Ethan," I admitted.

"Well, it's like this," Sam said. "Guys aren't possessions. No one can 'steal' him away from you. If he really likes you, then he's yours. If he doesn't and he goes to another girl just because she flirts with him, then he wasn't worth having, anyway."

I folded my arms. "Do you really believe that?"

"Well, no," she admitted. "The only person I know

mature enough to believe that is Carrie. It sounds great, though, doesn't it?"

"Yeah," I agreed wistfully. "But I don't have enough experience with boys to know what to do or how to act."

"Oh well, not to worry," Sam said breezily. "I have tons of experience with boys and I never know what to do or how to act, either! Night!"

SEVEN

"Graff!"

"Here!"

"Lebowitz!"

"Here!"

"Monroe!"

"Here!"

"Chernick!"

"Present!"

At six-fifteen the next morning, Liza called off the names of the kids going on the rafting trip, and one by one they got onto the bus. The staff milled around, waiting to make sure all the kids were aboard before we got on.

I automatically felt for my asthma inhaler in the back pocket of my shorts before sitting down. It was pure habit. It is so scary, that terrible feeling that I can't breathe. But as long as I have my inhaler, I know I'll be okay.

Although I hadn't had much sleep I was feeling

pretty excited. Ethan was standing right next to me, close enough to hold my hand even though he wasn't actually doing it at that exact moment.

"Okay, counselors, listen up!" Liza called to us once all the kids were on the bus. "Once we're aboard, Dee Dee is going to give out the raft assignments, and Kendra, our white-water rafting expert, will explain just how everything works."

Kendra, an attractive, super-fit-looking African-American girl with a beautiful, long braid, waved to us.

"This is our first trip away from camp," Liza continued, "and I want it to be a terrific success. Remember that we are in charge of these kids every minute, and I expect you all to take the responsibility very seriously. Any questions?"

"I have one," Tori said loudly. "Do all these kids need to know how to swim?"

Liza turned to Kendra for a reply.

"It doesn't really matter," Kendra said. "Everyone will have a life jacket on, and the level of rapids we're going won't require any swimming. However, Dee Dee divided up the raft assignments to make sure that there is one certified junior or senior lifeguard on each raft, just to be extra careful."

"Are you certified?" I asked Ethan casually.

"No," Ethan replied. "There was this great swimming teacher on the island, Kurt Ackerman, and he was going to train me for certification, but he split when he had this huge fight with Emma."

"Emma Cresswell?" I asked with surprise.

Ethan nodded. "It was a major scandal. See, what happened was—"

"Okay, all aboard," Liza yelled. "We're moving out!"

"Well, I'll finish the story later. By the way, are you certified?" Ethan asked me, as we waited in line to board the bus.

"Yes," I admitted shyly.

Ethan grinned. "Well, I guess that means I can be on your raft, huh?"

I grinned back. "I guess."

I climbed on the bus and immediately I heard her voice.

"Dixie! Dixie! Dixie! Sit with me! Over here! I saved your place!"

Patti.

Most of the kids were already sitting two to a seat, but there sat Patti by herself, her hand draped over the other half of the cushion, reserved for yours truly.

Not that any of the kids would have wanted to sit there, anyway.

What could I do? I sat with her.

She gave me a huge hug and actually kissed me wetly on the cheek. I resisted the urge to rub it off.

Ethan climbed on the bus after me, and he saw that

I was sitting with Patti, so he casually sat across from me, in the aisle seat. It was as close as we could get to each other under the circumstances.

The twins got on the bus and took in the scene. Patti still had her arms locked around my neck in a death grip. They rolled their eyes and climbed to the back of the bus. Tori got on and sat up front with Jodie. Then Dee Dee got on the bus. She looked at Ethan, looked at me, and smugly squeezed her way into the seat next to Ethan, practically falling in his lap.

"Is it okay if I sit with you?" she asked flirtatiously.

"Oh, sure," he replied, sort of laughing. "Do I have a choice?" He moved over to give her more room.

"You don't need to move so far away," Dee Dee told him. "I don't bite."

"I wouldn't bet on it," I said under my breath.

The bus driver started the bus, and some kids began singing camp songs. Patti squeezed me again tightly.

"This is going to be so fun, isn't it, Dixie?" she asked me happily.

"Does that mean rafting is one of the few things you don't think is stupid?" I asked her, still in a tiff over Dee Dee.

"But I'll be with you!" Patti exclaimed.

I looked over at her. "It's good that you're not afraid

of the water, after what happened at the pool your first day of camp."

Patti's eyes grew troubled. "Well, you saved me, didn't you? And you'll be with me this time, too."

"Just please be really careful," I told her.

"Okay, I'll hold your hand," Patti said, and proceeded to do just that.

Dee Dee chatted up Ethan, finding every excuse she could think of to touch his arm or his leg. And she'd turn to give me a smug look now and then. Patti continued to hold my hand in her sweaty grasp.

My friends were going to have to come to my rescue, or this trip was going to be just hopeless!

"Okay, listen up for your raft assignments," Dee Dee called to us. She stopped a moment to adjust the strap on her black bikini top, and then looked down at her clipboard. "There are six people to a raft, with at least one certified junior or senior lifesaver on each raft."

I held my fingers behind my back and crossed them superstitiously. *Please let her put me with Ethan. Please.*

She read out the first two raft assignments. I wasn't on either one. Neither was Ethan. So far, so good.

"Raft number three," Dee Dee continued. "The counselors are Dixie and Dwayne Urlee, the campers are Jodie, Sarah, Randy, and Patti." She looked up from her list and gave me a nasty grin.

"Hurrah!" Patti yelled, actually jumping into the air. "I knew I'd be with you! I just knew it!"

I was doomed.

Dee Dee continued her lists, which put the twins together on a raft with some of the nicer kids, and Tori with Pete Tilly. "Number six raft—the last one," Dee Dee called out. "The counselors will be me and Ethan Hewitt, and the campers are Mandi, Jennifer, Jake, and Anne-Marie."

I looked over at Ethan. He shrugged glumly.

Ethan was going to spend the day with Dee Dee.

I wasn't just doomed. I was double doomed.

"Hey, Randy, have fun with Porky Pink Stuff!" a boy called across the group. "She'll probably sink your raft!"

"Okay, folks, listen up!" Kendra called out in a loud voice. "Here's how it's gonna work. First, when I'm talking, no one else is talking. Am I understood?"

We all nodded our heads in compliance.

"Good," she said. "Because you have to respect the river at all times."

I looked at the Saco River, which was flowing past where we were standing. It was as smooth as glass, and when I'd dunked my hand in it earlier, the water was lukewarm.

"Now, it's time to put on your life vests," Kendra advised.

The counselors retrieved the life vests from the storage area under the bus and helped the campers put them on.

"Keep those vests on at all times," Kendra warned. "No joking around."

Of course, it was up to me to put Patti Chernick into her life vest. The life vest was bright orange. Patti was wearing a bright pink and red horizontally striped T-shirt. It was quite a sight.

"Okay," Kendra said. "The main thing to do is let the river do the work. We'll be in inflatable rubber rafts and you'll each have a paddle. But you don't actually have to do any paddling until we get to the white water. I've already briefed the staff on how to keep you on course."

The day before we'd had a meeting with Kendra, and she'd given us basic training for the rafting trip.

"White water!" Randy Blackson yelled with excitement. "Totally awesome!"

I looked over at Patti. She was beginning to get that green look on her face.

"Are you okay?" I whispered to her.

"I'm not sure. Maybe I ate too many donuts for breakfast."

I sighed and prayed we weren't in for an episode of barf city, even before we were on the raft.

"These are really easy rapids," Kendra continued.

"Boooo!" Jake O'Henry yelled. "No weenie rapids!"

"I didn't say they were weenie rapids," Kendra said, giving him a hard look. "And that is a bad and dangerous attitude. The water can be your friend and the water can also kill. It's all about respect. Have you got that?"

Jake nodded, looking somewhat cowed.

"Now, we won't really be getting into the white water until after lunch," Kendra explained. "Just remember, when we hit the rapids, paddle hard, because that makes it easier to control the raft."

"Hey, can some of us stay on shore and have you, like, mail us a video of the experience?" Jodie asked, making a nervous joke.

"No one has to go," Liza said. "You all signed up because you wanted to go."

"Hey, I was kidding. Lighten up," Jodie replied. She tossed her hair out of her eyes. "What if we hit a rock, though?"

"Well, you'll bounce off," Kendra said wryly. "That's why the rafts are made out of rubber."

"What if we fall out of the raft?" Sarah Sloan asked.

"You won't," Kendra replied. "But if you do, just

keep your head up and your feet down. The life vests will keep you up. Any other questions?"

There were none.

"Okay, have fun, follow the rules, respect the water," Kendra said. "Now you can carry your rafts into the water."

Dee Dee moved closer to Ethan, making sure I was watching her. "Oh, Ethan," she said, "I hope you know mouth-to-mouth resuscitation, just in case I need it," she purred.

"Yeah, kind of," Ethan replied, looking embarrassed.

Becky was standing next to me, taking in the exchange between Dee Dee and Ethan. "Let's drown her like the rat she is," Becky suggested.

Allie came up next to her sister. "Hey, Brittany from the blue team told me that last night she saw Dee Dee with Pete Tilly at the Play Café acting very friendly, if you catch my drift."

"How friendly?" I asked.

"Well, let's just say you couldn't tell where her lips ended and his began," Allie reported.

"So why is she flirting with Ethan?" I asked my friends with frustration. "She's fifteen! She doesn't really care a thing about him!"

"Just to tick you off, is my guess," Becky said. "Also maybe it'll make Pete jealous, which would make her really happy."

"I bet she put Pete with Tori because she thinks Tori is totally safe," Allie put in. "Like Pete could never like Tori."

I sighed. "Maybe I'll get to be with Ethan at lunch, at least. Dee Dee can't do anything about that."

"Hey, girls, let's hustle!" Liza called to us. "Get those rafts in the water!"

"See ya downstream," Becky called to me, hurrying off.

"This is going to be the most fun ever," Patti said as we dragged our raft into the calm water. "Hey, how about if we sing every verse of 'A Hundred Bottles of Beer on the Wall'?" she asked the other kids on our raft with excitement.

"How about if we don't and say we did," was Jodie's retort. She climbed into the raft and grabbed her paddle. "Now what?"

Dwayne and I made sure our four kids were settled in the raft, then we both climbed in, me in front, him in the back.

"Now we float," I told Jodie, pushing us off lightly.

In front of us I could see Dee Dee and Ethan's raft, gently floating along with the current. Dee Dee looked me right in the eye, and then she leaned forward, grabbed Ethan's hand, and squeezed it tightly. At the same moment, Patti grabbed my hand and held it just as tight.

I sighed and stared longingly at Ethan, who was looking down at the bottom of the raft like he wasn't sure what had happened.

EIGHT

"Twenty-seven bottles of beer on the wall
Twenty-seven bottles of beer!
If one of those bottles should happen to fall
There'll be twenty-six bottles of beer on the wall!"

We'd been in the raft for over three hours and had only gone over one tiny little rapid. Patti had been singing for the past hour at the top of her lungs. Take my word for it. She had very strong lungs.

I was seriously considering drowning myself as a viable option.

"Hey, how about if I teach you kids a different song?" Dwayne asked when Patti took a breath, heading into the next verse.

"After I finish this one," Patti replied.

"I thought you told me you don't like music," Jodie said darkly.

"I like camp songs," Patti explained. "Also musical theater. I thought you were talking about the kind of music you hear on MTV or something."

"I was," Jodie confirmed.

"I'm not even allowed to watch MTV," Patti said with a shrug.

Yet another thing Patti and I had in common. I wasn't allowed to watch MTV either. Which only meant I watched it every chance I could at my friends' houses.

"Hey, I can sing the entire score to 'Oklahoma,'" Patti said eagerly. "Want to hear me?"

"It beats 'A Hundred Bottles of Beer on the Wall,'" Sarah said with a sigh. She gave me a pleading look. "Can't you make her stop?"

"This is the first song in the show," Patti reported. "It's called 'Oh, What a Beautiful Morning.'"

I couldn't take it. Not another minute of it. I knew I wasn't being sweet and my mother would have a fit, but my mother wasn't there, was she?

"Patti!" I yelled, grabbing her arm. "Hush!"

She stared at me, her huge eyes round and luminous.

"Just hush up!" I cried. "There are five people in this raft besides you. And those five people don't want to hear you sing anymore!"

She bit her lower lip. "Sorry," she said quietly.

Immediately I hated myself.

"It's okay," I said gently. "I'm glad you're so happy and all. But you need to try and be a little more considerate of others, okay?"

She pretended to zip up her lip and then threw the imaginary key into the water.

"Thank you, God," Jodie mumbled.

"We're breaking for lunch!" Liza called from the raft in front of us. "Counselors and C.I.T.s jump out first, right by those big rocks!"

The raft was moving very slowly, and Dwayne and I jumped out, followed by the campers. Patti tripped over a rock and almost fell in the water, but I caught her.

"You okay?" I asked her.

She pointed to her still zipped lip, as if to say she couldn't talk. I considered it a blessing.

Some of the staff unloaded packs of food from the rafts. Becky, Allie, and Pete began to unpack them on the nearby picnic tables.

"Don't go too far into those woods!" Liza called to some kids who were running up an incline toward the trees. "Counselors, watch your campers! Get a head count!"

"All our kids are here," I told Dwayne as he pulled a cooler of lemonade off our raft. I went over to the picnic tables and set up some paper cups and the plastic pitchers of lemonade. I casually looked around for Ethan, trying not to let it appear that I was looking for him, if you know what I mean.

And there he was, looking for me. Our eyes met, he smiled and strolled over.

"Hi," he said, putting one leg up on the picnic bench.

"Hey," I replied, as I put out a stack of napkins. "Having fun?"

"Yeah, the river is cool," Ethan said. "I'd like to see some real white water, though."

"I didn't necessarily mean the water," I said meaningfully, glancing over at Dee Dee, who was going over a list of something with Liza.

He looked over at her and blushed. "Oh, well, she's okay. She knows a lot about rafting."

"Come and get it!" Pete called out.

All the kids began to yell and scream, running wildly toward the picnic tables piled high with sandwiches, chips, and fruit.

"Oh, that's very helpful, Pete," Liza said sarcastically. She blew the whistle around her neck hard. "Form a line by that tree!" Liza yelled, pointing to a small evergreen a couple feet from the picnic tables. "We're going to do this in an orderly fashion, or no one eats!"

"We might as well wait until the line is smaller," I said to Ethan.

He nodded, and we walked away from the picnic tables. I saw Patti in line for lunch talking with Jodie. Or rather Patti was talking; Jodie was suffering.

This was my chance to get away from Patti. The only thing she loved more than me was food.

Ethan and I strolled toward the trees. I picked a leaf off a low branch and twirled it in my fingers. Back over at the picnic tables, I saw Dee Dee walk up behind Pete and put her arms around him from behind. I could see him looking over his shoulder, laughing and talking with her.

"Dee Dee's going out with Pete Tilly," I told Ethan casually.

"Oh, yeah?" he asked, looking over at them. He folded his arms. "She's kind of a flirt," he added.

"So, do you like that?" I asked, not looking at him.

"Not really," he replied. "It's kind of lame, you know?"

Now I did look at him. "I think so, too.

"Want to go into the woods?" I asked him boldly. My mother would just up and die if she heard me ask a boy that. I didn't plan to tell her.

"Sure," Ethan said, and we walked a little ways into the woods. "It's really nice here, huh? Peaceful."

"And quiet," I added. "No noisy campers."

"No noisy Dee Dee," Ethan said with a laugh. He picked up a stone and threw it through the trees. "She kept going on and on about how much trouble she got into at her boarding school in Switzerland. Like I care."

"She was just trying to impress you, I'll bet," I said.

"Why bother?" Ethan asked. "I mean, she's fifteen and a total babe. It would be different if she really liked me, but I don't guess she does," he added, pushing some hair off his forehead.

"Do you wish she did?"

He shrugged. "She's cute."

"So's a kitten," I said sweetly, "but that doesn't mean she won't claw and shed and mess the furniture."

Ethan laughed. "She's definitely not as funny as you are."

"Good," I said primly.

"And not as smart," he added.

"Also good," I said, starting to smile.

"All and all, I'd say I like you a lot better," he finished in a low voice.

"Really?" I asked. I could feel my whole face lighting up.

"Really," he echoed in a low voice.

He turned to me, and I looked up at him. We were standing so close I could smell the peppermint from the gum he'd been chewing.

And at that moment I knew. I just knew. He was going to kiss me.

I lifted my chin and closed my eyes, ready for the moment I had dreamt about, wondered about, and secretly practiced for with my pillow at night.

His lips were just about on mine, everything was perfect, when suddenly, there she was.

"Dixie! Dixie! I brought you some food!" Patti yelled, stumbling through the trees toward us.

Ethan and I jumped apart guiltily.

"I saw you guys walk back here, and—" Patti stumbled and went down, the paper plate of food falling into the underbrush.

"You okay?" Ethan asked, helping her up.

"Oh, yeah, sure," Patti said.

"Why did you follow me?" I asked her, trying to control my anger.

"Well, I wanted to bring you some lunch and—"

"I'm perfectly capable of getting my own lunch!" I yelled. "What I want is some privacy!"

She took a step backwards, looking frightened. "My stomach might be upset. . . ."

"Too bad!" I yelled. "Stop eating if your stomach gets upset! Go make a friend! Go talk to a tree! Just please leave me alone for five minutes!"

Patti's jaw fell open in shock. Her lower lip trembled, then she turned and ran back toward the picnic tables.

I couldn't believe what I had just done.

"Patti, wait!" I called to her. "I'm sorry! I didn't mean it!"

But it was too late. She was gone.

95

NINE

"Okay, campers, listen up. We have some important announcements about this afternoon's rafting, which is when we'll be running into some true white water!" Liza called out to us after lunch. "First we're doing a head count, so call out when I read your name."

One half of my mind was listening to Liza, and the other half was watching Patti, who sat by herself under a tree. She was refusing to speak to me and hadn't said a word when I'd tried to apologize to her.

"Hey, chill," Becky whispered to me, nudging me hard. She was sitting next to me at a picnic table, and she saw how I kept looking over at Patti. When I came out of the woods with Ethan, I'd had a chance to briefly tell my friends what had happened and they all thought I was making too big a thing about yelling at Patti.

"I'm a slug," I whispered back to Becky. "I'm lower than that—a bug on a slug. I never should have yelled at her."

"I'm just amazed you didn't do it sooner," Allie whispered from the other side of me. "We're really sorry we couldn't stop Patti from chasing you into the woods. I mean, we didn't even see her disappear!"

"Yeah, one second she was in the lunch line, and then she was gone," Becky added.

"Oh, it's not y'all's fault," I assured them. "I'm the one that messed up."

"You don't have to try to be so perfect all the time, you know," Tori said, scratching a mosquito bite on her leg. "Hey, what did it feel like to kiss Ethan, anyway?"

I looked over at Ethan, who was sitting with the group from his raft, and I sighed. "It was more an about-to-happen kiss than an actual kiss," I explained. Dee Dee laughed at something Ethan said, and she leaned her head against his shoulder. "Oh! Look at that!"

"She is the biggest flirt in the world," Allie said.

"Ethan thinks she's cute," I reported forlornly.

"Well, she is," Tori pointed out honestly.

"Okay, let's talk about white water," Kendra said in a loud voice. "Remember, when you get to the rapids, everyone paddles. Keep the weight in the boat evenly distributed. Don't fool around. Don't stand up."

"We'll be going through one gentle white-water section," Liza continued, "and then one serious one. After that we pretty much coast down to the end.

Then we'll cart our rafts up the path to the road and load out."

"Cart the rafts?" Jake repeated. "You mean, like, carry them on our backs?"

"They're not heavy, Jake," Liza said patiently.

"Well, why can't the bus just come pick us up at the river?" Pete Tilly asked.

"Because there is no road there," Liza answered. "We'll hike about a half mile and we'll be at the bus."

"No one said anything about hiking," another kid groused.

"Hey, these rich kids are kind of spoiled, you know?" Tori said.

"Hiking won't hurt you a bit," Liza told the kid. "Okay, let's move it out!"

"See you at the end," I called to my friends, as they scattered to get their rafts. Dwayne and I got the kids together and dragged our raft back into the water. Patti helped, but she wouldn't look at me or talk to me.

Once our raft was floating, I decided to try again.

"How long are you going to be mad at me?" I asked her.

She shrugged.

"Friends forgive friends, don't they?"

She gave me a hard look. "You're not my friend. You just pretended to be."

"That's not true!" I cried, even though what she was saying really was true.

"I'm very smart, so you don't have to pretend anymore," Patti said. "I don't know why I thought you could ever like me."

"But I do like you!" I protested guiltily.

"No, you don't," Patti said in a flat voice. "I was stupid to think you did. You're perfect. Why would you like me?"

"Oh, Patti, I'm not perfect," I said with a sigh. "I'm really, truly so far from perfect." The sun caught the light in my diamond tennis bracelet, which gave me an idea. "You know this bracelet I wear all the time?"

She looked at it. "What about it?"

"My dad gave it to me a year ago after I got out of the hospital."

"For what?" Patti asked, still staring at the bracelet.

"I have asthma," I explained to Patti. "And I had a really bad asthma attack. I couldn't breathe, and I ended up in the hospital. It was such a scary feeling—sucking for air and not being able to get enough. And after that I was so scared that I didn't want to do anything—play sports, ride my bike—because I was so afraid I'd have another asthma attack."

"So, what happened?" Patti asked, interested in spite of herself.

"Well, my father gave me this bracelet," I explained, turning it around slowly on my wrist. "And he told me it would protect me. As long as I wore it, he said I'd always be able to breathe."

"That's stupid," Patti said flatly.

"Oh, I know," I agreed. "But it helped me to not be so afraid. I've worn it ever since, and I haven't been back to the hospital."

Patti looked at me sideways. "I'd rather have terrible, awful asthma than be fat and ugly and have everyone hate me."

I was quiet for a moment. "Feeling sorry for yourself won't change anything," I finally said. "Maybe if you—"

"White water ahead!" Dwayne called.

We paddled through the gentle white water, the raft swiftly flowing over the churning water.

"That was fun," Patti said in a small voice, a slight smile on her face.

I was so happy to see her grinning that I impetuously undid the bracelet on my arm. "How about if I loan this to you for the rest of the trip?" I said.

Her eyes got huge. "Why would you do that? That bracelet means so much to you."

"Because you're my friend," I said.

"I don't think you should trust me," Patti replied. "I mess up too much. That's what my parents say. That's what everyone says."

"No, you don't," I said firmly. I put the bracelet in

her hand, and I felt really good about it. "Friends share," I said quietly.

"I don't have anything to share with you," Patti said.

"You do," I insisted. "People like people who are nice to them and are considerate of their feelings, and who don't think about themselves all the time. You could be more like that, and you could share it with me."

I quickly fastened my bracelet onto her wrist. It fit much more snugly on her than on me, but it looked really nice.

"I'm sorry I showed up when Ethan was kissing you," Patti whispered, staring at the bottom of the raft.

"It's okay," I assured her, reaching over and giving her arm a squeeze. "I'm sorry I yelled at you."

"White water up ahead!" Dwayne called out again. "Heads up, folks! This is the real thing!"

"Okay, we all paddle steady!" I called to the kids on our raft. I looked up in front at the churning, tumbling water and a thrill of excitement tore up my spine.

"Here we gooooo!" Dwayne cried as we hit the white water.

We all paddled steadily as our raft bounced and slipped over the teeming water. The kids screamed with glee.

"Hey, this is fun!" Patti cried, looking over at me.

She lifted her paddle out of the water and the raft began to list to the left.

"Paddle!" I yelled at her.

She was startled, and the paddle almost slipped out of her hand. She grabbed it at the last minute, but the end of the paddle got caught underneath my diamond bracelet. Meanwhile, the raft veered dangerously to the left, toward the rocks.

"Paddle, you fat idiot!" Randy screamed at Patti, his face white with fear.

I reached over and tried to help her, but a spray of water hit that jostled me hard. I fell back into the raft.

"Quit moving around!" Dwayne screamed.

"Just pull the paddle out!" I called to Patti. She struggled to get the end of the paddle out from under the bracelet. She pulled against it frantically, and I saw the bracelet pop and go flying off into the water.

No, no, she couldn't have just broken and lost my lucky bracelet! But she had!

"Oh, Dixie, I'm so sorry!" Patti yelled over the sounds of the rushing water.

"Just keep paddling," I said through clenched teeth. There was nothing I could do. My bracelet was lost. If my father found out, he would kill me first and ask questions later.

We were through the white water. Everything grew

quiet except for the sounds of the happy kids, excited from their adventure.

"Please don't hate me," Patti pleaded with me tearfully.

"I don't hate you," I replied in a low voice. I didn't even sound convincing to myself, because at that moment I'd have liked to kill her.

"How could I do it?" Patti asked herself, and as she said that, she smacked herself in the forehead, causing her baseball cap to fall off into the water. The wind picked up, blowing the cap to my side of the raft, where it skittered over the surface.

"I'll get it," I told Patti, reaching out for her hat.

"No, it's okay. I can get it," Patti insisted. "You don't have to be nice to me anymore." She leaned over me, grabbing for her hat. The raft hit a swell in the water, and Patti fell into me from behind.

"Oof!" Patti uttered, reaching out to steady herself. But instead she hit my back, pushing against it and sending me headlong out of the raft. I tumbled into the river, more shocked than anything.

"Girl overboard!" Patti yelled frantically. "Girl overboard!"

I bobbed alongside the raft in my bright orange life vest.

"You okay?" Dwayne asked, reaching out for me.

"Yeah, just hoist me back in," I told him. Dwayne

lifted me back into the raft and I lay there, soaking wet, dripping on everything.

"You guys okay back there?" Kendra called from her raft.

"I'm fine," I yelled back with embarrassment.

"It's my fault, isn't it?" Patti said.

"Yes," I snapped.

She hovered over me. "Want me to . . . wipe you off or something?"

"No. Don't do anything at all," I told her in a steely voice.

We traveled along for five minutes or so, and the water became gentle and calm. I could see that it was getting shallower as the bottom became visible. I just sat there feeling miserable, dripping, mourning the loss of my magic tennis bracelet, embarrassed about falling in the water, and ticked off at Patti about everything.

"Okay, counselors!" Liza yelled. "When we get down the river another thousand feet or so—by that grove of pine trees—jump out and drag the rafts over to the shore!"

"You got that, Dixie?" Dwayne asked me.

I nodded, but I was only half listening. Because a funny thing was happening. A feeling I hadn't had in quite a while—that little feeling in the back of my throat that told me an asthma attack was coming.

"Dixie?" Patti asked.

No, it couldn't be an asthma attack. I refused to have an asthma attack. I was just being superstitious because my tennis bracelet was gone.

"Dixie? Dixie? Please talk to me!" Patti cried.

I breathed shallowly, concentrating on each breath. In. Out. In. Out. I knew I shouldn't get excited. Getting excited was the worst thing I could do. If the feeling lasted, I would just use my inhaler—it didn't matter if it was embarrassing to use it in front of everyone.

"I'm so sorry I made you fall into the river," Patti said. "And I'll buy you a new tennis bracelet, just like the one you had. I'll make my parents give me the money."

Dixie, get a hold of yourself, I told myself. *You only think you're having an asthma attack because your lucky bracelet is gone. Well, it isn't really magic, so just stop being so danged silly about this.*

In. Out. In. Out.

Well, I knew it was dumb to be embarrassed about using the inhaler. I just hated it when everyone asked a million questions about it. But I knew I had to pull it out and get a few blasts of it into my lungs.

I reached into my back pocket.

My inhaler was gone.

TEN

But that couldn't be. I had *definitely* put it there. It *had* to be there.

I felt for it again. I could picture it in my head, nestled inside its plastic waterproof case with the little loop of cord that makes it easier to carry.

No inhaler.

"You ready to drag the raft?" Dwayne called to me.

"Sure," I said quickly in a soft voice, because what else could I do? I jumped out of the raft, breathing shallowly, and helped drag the raft to shore.

Then I sat down hard. And concentrated on breathing.

"Dixie?" Dwayne asked, putting his hands on his knees and peering at me. "You okay?"

I shook my head in the negative. "I . . . think I have a little problem," I managed to get out. "I . . . have asthma. And I lost my inhaler. And . . . I need it."

Dwayne looked alarmed. "You can't breathe?"

"Not too well," I admitted.

"Just sit tight," Dwayne told me, and he ran over to Liza.

"Oh my God, oh my God," Patti cried, clapping her hand over her mouth. "Where's your inhaler?"

"It . . . must have fallen out of my pocket when I fell in the water. . . ." Now I was sucking air, gasping for breath. How could this possibly be happening to me?

Liza ran over to me. "Dix?"

"No inhaler," I managed. Liza knew I had asthma. It was on my health report when I had applied to be a C.I.T. I could feel my bronchial tubes constricting. I was trying not to panic, but I felt so scared.

Tori, Becky, and Allie came running over. They huddled around me, holding my hand.

"We have to get her to the hospital!" Patti screamed. "She can't breathe!"

"The bus is a half mile up that hill," Liza snapped. "She can't get to it." Liza looked right into my eyes. "Do you know where you lost the inhaler?"

"Must have . . . been when I . . . fell out of the boat," I gasped.

"It was right back there, where that big tree dips into the water," Patti said, pointing back up the river. "See, my hat is stuck back there in the branches."

"Don't you have a first aid kit with something in it

that will help her?" Becky cried, holding my hand tightly.

"She told me she always carried her own inhaler," Liza said, panic in her eyes. She took a deep breath, then she looked over at Kendra. "Okay, here's the plan. We can't move Dixie. I'm going to run up the hill to the bus, and get the driver to drive to the nearest hospital for an inhaler. Meanwhile, you're going to have to dive to try and find the one she lost."

"It's a long shot," I heard Kendra tell Liza in a low voice.

"Well, it may be the only shot we have," Liza replied. She stroked the hair off my forehead. "Lay down, honey," she told me gently. "I'll run as fast as I can and get you some help."

"Let me go," Tori begged. "I run faster than you do."

"Okay," Liza decided, grabbing Tori's arm hard. "Run like your life depended on it."

"I love you, Dixie," Tori whispered, and then she took off up the hill.

"I'll stay with her," Ethan said, and I felt myself being carefully pulled down so that my head was in Ethan's lap.

"I . . . feel . . . so . . . dumb," I managed, staring up into his eyes.

"Shhhh," he said, staring down at me. "You're gonna be okay, Dix."

"Okay, I need excellent swimmers and divers only

to swim with me to that hanging tree," Kendra barked out in a no-nonsense voice.

Becky, Allie, and two other counselors stood up.

"My sister has asthma," Pete Tilly said. "The container for her inhaler floats—it popped out of her bathing suit once at the beach. Does yours?"

I managed to nod.

"Good deal," Kendra said. "Maybe we'll get lucky." She stood up. "Everyone else search down here in the water, in case the inhaler floats downstream."

Everyone but Ethan, Patti, and Liza waded into the water. Kendra and the other strong swimmers began to swim upstream.

"I want to go, too," Patti said quickly, jumping up.

"Forget it," Liza snapped. "You practically drowned your first day of camp. You can't swim."

"Yes, I can," Patti said in a quavery voice. "I can swim really well. And I can hold my breath underwater a really, really long time, too."

We all stared at her.

"I wasn't really drowning," she admitted with tears in her eyes. "I did it so Dixie would save me. And then I had to keep pretending I couldn't swim after that."

"I don't believe it," Ethan muttered with disgust.

"I don't care what you think," Patti shot back at him. "But I can help. And I'm going to."

"Patti, wait—" Liza called.

But Patti wasn't listening. She jumped into the

water and began to swim quickly, with a strong, determined stroke.

"I can't believe she pretended to drown," Liza said.

"Seriously lame," Ethan added.

In. Out. In. Out.

It was all I could do to concentrate on the little air I could manage to suck into my lungs. They were burning, and still I couldn't manage to suck enough air into them. I could feel myself getting sleepy, my mind traveling to another place.

"Don't let her go to sleep!" Liza yelled. She crouched down next to me. "Dixie! Don't pass out! You can't pass out!"

I was wheezing now, fighting with my tortured lungs. "I . . . can't . . . breathe!" I gasped.

"Hey, I think I see it!" Becky yelled from far away, treading water. She dove down and I waited and prayed as hard as I could.

"I can see it," she said, sputtering as she came up. "But the loop is caught under a rock. I'm diving for it!"

In the distance I could just barely make out Becky disappearing under the water. After a while she came back up, gasping for air. "I can't hold my breath long enough to get it free!"

"I can!" I heard Patti cry. "Let me!"

"Wait!" Kendra yelled. "It isn't safe—"

Patti didn't listen. She dove.

111

"Just hang on, Dixie," Ethan said, stroking my hair.
It seemed like forever. No one was talking.

In. Out. In. Out.

Please, God, please, let them find my inhaler.

My eyes fluttered and closed. I couldn't do it anymore.

"Oh my God, she's turning blue!" someone cried.

I knew it must be me they were talking about, but everything seemed so far away.

"I got it!" I heard Patti yell in the distance. "It was stuck under a rock and I got it!"

Everyone started cheering, crying, and applauding. The next thing I knew Kendra was there dripping on me and putting the inhaler in my hand. Quickly I squeezed it into my mouth, pulling at the air hard.

Nothing ever felt so good in my life.

I used the inhaler again, taking it deep into my lungs. I could breathe! I could breathe again! Becky and Allie threw their arms around me and hugged me hard.

"Don't go scaring us like that, you bozo," Allie said fervently. "It isn't funny."

"That was scarier than a Stephen King novel," Becky added.

"Dixie?" Patti asked in a little voice. She stood near the shore, looking like a small, round, miserable little sea creature.

"Thank you," I said to her. "You saved my life."

She walked over to me. "But it was my fault in the first place," she protested.

"I'd say a number of mistakes were made here," Liza said briskly. "I should have had an extra inhaler in the first aid kit. I'm sorry."

I breathed in and out. It felt so wonderful. Never again would I take breathing for granted.

"Thank you, all of you, for being so wonderful," I managed to say.

"Hey," Jodie said to Patti, her hands on her hips. "I thought you couldn't swim. I was sitting right next to you at the pool when you fell in and almost drowned."

"Yeah, that's right," Jake agreed. "What's with you, anyway?"

Everyone turned and stared at Patti.

"I . . . I only pretended to drown," she admitted to everyone.

"Excuse me," Jodie said, "but that is the stupidest thing I ever heard in my life."

"I know," Patti agreed, biting at her lower lip. "I just wanted some attention, I guess. I was really nervous that day. It was stupid. I'm sorry."

"Hey, Patti just saved my life," I reminded the group. "That counts for a lot."

Liza helped me up and I took Patti's hands. "You did great, Patti."

Her eyes shone brightly. "I couldn't stand it if anything happened to you. You're the only one who's ever nice to me."

"Well, since when have you been nice to anyone else at this camp?" Sarah piped up, staring at Patti, her hands on her hips.

"Yeah, we'd like you if you were nicer," Jennifer added. "But you're always saying everything is stupid, and you always know better than everyone else, and you're always telling everyone how smart you are. . . ."

"It's obnoxious," Jodie concluded.

"I know," Patti agreed miserably. She pushed some wet hair out of her eyes. "Everyone hates me."

"And that's another thing!" Jake exclaimed. "Why are you feeling sorry for yourself all the time?"

"Why do you guys make fun of me all the time?" Patti countered, sticking up for herself.

"Okay, okay, enough of this," Liza said. "I think we're all grateful for what Patti just did for Dixie. And I think you guys can all work on being nicer and kinder to each other. Right?"

Some kids nodded, others stood their ground and looked cynical.

Liza turned to me. "Do you think you can walk to the road? Should we get you checked out at the hospital?"

"I can walk," I told her. "And I'm breathing okay now."

"Well, just take it slow and easy. And if you feel sick or anything just let me know and we'll stop and take a rest."

"Okay," I agreed.

"I'm gonna stay right next to you and make sure you're okay," Ethan told me softly. He took my hand and I smiled at him. Becky and Allie noticed. Becky winked at me and Allie gave me the thumbs-up sign.

Slowly we climbed up the path to the road. Once I felt tired and I stopped for a few minutes and used the inhaler again, but then I was fine. And Ethan kept our hands firmly entwined the whole way.

The bus and Tori weren't back yet, so we sat down by the side of the road to wait. I sat on the edge of the raft with Ethan. Patti came running over to us.

"Hey, Dixie, guess what?" she asked with excitement. "Sarah just invited me over to her house! We're gonna have a hold-your-breath contest in the pool in her backyard!"

"That's wonderful!" I told her.

"She's the same age as me," Patti went on, her words rushing out. "Maybe she wants to be friends!"

"I'm sure she does," I agreed. "I'm sure that's why she invited you. Now, all you have to do is to be a good friend to her."

"I will. I promise!" Patti vowed. "I remember what

you told me about how a real friend acts, and I can do it."

"I know you can," I agreed. She turned to Ethan. "I'm sorry I walked into the woods right when you were going to kiss Dixie," she said in a loud voice.

Some kids sitting near us tittered, others *ooooed* and made lip-smacking noises, and Ethan blushed.

"It's okay," Ethan mumbled.

"Well, I won't do that again," Patti promised, seeming oblivious of how embarrassed Ethan and I felt. "I mean, you can kiss her anytime! You could kiss her now if you wanted!"

I wanted to crawl under the raft and die of embarrassment.

But then to my surprise, Ethan laughed. "Good idea," he said.

And the next thing I knew, Ethan's lips were on mine, and in front of everyone on that rafting trip, he kissed me.

A real, true kiss.

It was wonderful. Much better than my pillow.

Kids began to whoop and holler, some of them applauded and I was blushing and grinning. Ethan was too, but it was okay, because he put his arm around me and held me tight.

Someone turned on a portable radio and music blared out. The sun still shone high in the sky. My friends Becky and Allie were boogying to the beat

116

right by me. My other friend Tori would be back any minute. And I had just been kissed by Ethan Hewitt in front of everyone. The entire summer stretched before me, full of endless possibilities.

Y'all, it was the greatest moment of my life.

appears in stores. Hope this helps to clear things up!

Best,
Cherie

Dear Cherie,

I really enjoyed the first Club Sunset Island book, Too Many Boys! At first I had my doubts that it would be as good as the regular Sunset Island books, but this book was great! I have a few questions. How do you decide on the names and actions of your characters? When is your next book coming out? I can't wait to read the next Club Sunset Island book!

Your biggest fan,
Kelly Weiper
Kelseyville, California

Dear Kelly,

I just make up the names the same way you would if you were writing a story. I have a friend named Dixie (she's little and blond and smart, just like this Dixie!) and I've always thought Tori was the cutest name. As for the actions of my characters, sometimes I take them from my own experiences or those of my friends, and sometimes I just make them up. I also get great ideas from readers, which I often use.

The next Club Sunset Island book is Tori's Crush, and it will be out in August. And the next Sunset Island book, due out at the same time, is Sunset Illusions. Whoa, am I busy!

Best,
Cherie

find it interesting to learn how much Becky and Allie admire Sam? They're just really insecure and afraid that she might not really care about them, or that she'll take off like their mother did. Kinda sad, huh?

Best,
Cherie

Dear Cherie,

Your new Club Sunset Island series is the best! I couldn't put Too Many Boys! down! I could really relate to the characters and problems in this book. It's great to read a book with believable problems! I also love how Becky, Allie, Dixie, and Tori stay best friends through thick and thin. Why does it take so long for a book you write to be printed? Please keep on writing.

Sara Ford
Tonica, Illinois

Dear Sara,

Here are the basics of the publishing process: I discuss the plot with my editor, write an outline, and then write the manuscript. My editor reads through and edits the book, and then sends it to another type of editor who checks for things like grammatical and spelling errors. After that, the manuscript goes into page proofs, which means the story is set in type and laid out the way you see it in the finished book. After that, my editor and I review it again, and then the book is printed, bound, and sent out to the book-stores. As you can see, there are many steps involved. A book is usually written at least six months before it joined the hundreds of thousands of other Sunset readers, it can be real for you, too. Thank you for being so wonderful!

See you on the island!
Best,
Cherie Bennett

Cherie Bennett
c/o General Licensing Company
24 West 25th Street
New York, New York 10010

All letters printed become property of the publisher.

Dear Cherie,

I really loved your new book, Too Many Boys! It was wonderful! It's about time there was a book about the younger teens on the island. Do Allie and Becky remind you of yourself when you were fourteen?

Lots of love,
Lisa Hurley
Lakewood, California

Dear Lisa,

I was not nearly as outspoken as Becky and Allie are when I was fourteen. Sometimes they say things I would have liked have said though! I really like the twins a lot. It was a blast writing from Becky's point of view in Too Many Boys! since we've only seen her from Sam's view in the Sunset Island books. Did you

CLUB SUNSET ISLAND MAILBOX

Dear Readers,

I loved writing Dixie's First Kiss. When my husband, Jeff, read it, he asked me about my first kiss. I was thirteen, and the boy's name was Joel. I was crazed for him. I used to write his name over and over in my notebooks. I sketched exactly what I was going to wear to a party where I knew I would see him. And then . . . The Party. There he was, looking perfect. I could hardly breathe. We all played Spin the Bottle. He got me. We kissed. I thought life was perfect. Until he called my best friend and told her he didn't really like me at all, which broke my heart.

Well, Joel, wherever you are, I am totally over you and now I'm a famous author and I'm married to a really cool, cute guy, so nah-nah! Well, if I were *really* over him I wouldn't even remember his name now would I? I guess rejection is never completely forgotten.

I have already received the greatest letters from readers of Club Sunset Island. Everyone seems to be psyched about the adventures of Becky, Allie, Dixie, and Tori. I really want to hear from the rest of you, so please write with your ideas and suggestions. I also love getting your photos, and I put them up in my office. You guys are the cutest! Don't forget to let me know if I can consider your letter for publication. Readers often ask me if Sunset Island is a real place. Alas, only in my mind. But now that you've